TALES FROM THE ARK

Mr Noah could not sleep. He lay in bed, listening to the wind howling round outside, and the snuffles and grunts of the animals inside, and he talked to God.

'Listen, God,' he said. 'It's not too late. You need a lion-tamer for this job, or a big game hunter, or at least a zoo keeper. I'm very grateful, of course, that you want to save me and my family, but honestly, I'm not cut out for the job.

'And I'll tell you something, God,' Mr Noah went on. 'I'm scared of spiders and we've got two on board.'

Spiders aren't Mr Noah's only problem. The lion wants to be in charge, the sheep goes missing and the animals threaten to revolt because of the smell from the skunks. Worst of all, the ark begins to leak.

AVRIL ROWLANDS worked for the BBC for many years and has written screenplays for children's television as well as books. She now works as a freelance writer and runs training courses in television production. Her hobbies include swimming, walking, theatre and steam railways. She lives with her husband near Stratford-upon-Avon, England.

My especial thanks to Leslie Guest
for his support, help and enthusiasm
in the writing of this book

Tales from the Ark

Avril Rowlands
Illustrations by Rosslyn Moran

A LION BOOK

Copyright © 1993 Avril Rowlands
Illustrations copyright © 1993 Rosslyn Moran

The author asserts the moral right
to be identified as the author of this work

Published by
Lion Publishing plc
850 North Grove Avenue, Elgin, Illinois 60120, USA
ISBN 0 7459 2375 5

First edition 1993
Reprinted 1993
First US edition 1995

Library of Congress Cataloging-in-Publication Data
applied for

Printed and bound in the USA

CONTENTS

1
NOAH'S TALE

Mr Noah was six hundred years old when God had a serious talk with him.

'It makes me very sad to have to say it, Mr Noah, but of all the people who live in this world I created, you are the only good one. I have been very patient, but there is so much wickedness and evil that I must do something about it. I shall make a fresh start.'

Mr Noah was upset when he heard this, but he had to admit that God was right.

'What are you going to do, God?' he asked.

God sighed. 'I am afraid that I shall have to destroy every living creature,' he said sadly. 'But I shall save you, Mr Noah, and your wife. I shall also save your three sons, Shem, Ham and Japheth and their wives. And I shall save two of all the living creatures in the world for they are all important. I shall be relying on you, Mr Noah, to look after them for me and keep them alive. This is what I want you to do ...'

Then God told Mr Noah how to build a wooden ark, which was like a large boat, so that when God sent a great flood to cover the earth, Mr Noah, his family and the animals could be saved.

Mr Noah was not much good at carpentry but his sons and daughters-in-law helped and the ark was built on time. They filled it with food of every kind and, on the great day, Mr Noah, a worried frown on his face and a long, long list in his hand, ticked off the animals as they entered the ark.

There were wild animals, tame animals, reptiles and insects, beasts and birds. There were large animals and small animals, ugly and good-looking ones. There were animals with nice natures and animals with nasty natures.

Two of each kind went into the ark, just as God had said to Mr Noah. There were, however, no fish, because fish do not need saving from a flood.

Once everyone was safely inside, God shut the door

behind them.

'Will the ark be watertight?' asked Mr Noah anxiously.

'Of course it will,' said God. 'Now stop worrying, Noah, and look after everyone well, for in seven days I shall send the rain.'

So Mr Noah went into the great hall inside the ark, and if he was worried before, now he was terrified.

For there were lions and tigers, llamas and giraffes, leopards and lizards, sheep and cows, horses and goats, donkeys, elephants, camels, monkeys, snakes, birds... in fact every animal you can think of, plus all the ones you cannot think of. And not just one, but *two* of each, and they were all milling around the great hall, arguing, fighting, squawking, screeching and making the most terrible noise that had ever been heard.

Mrs Noah and her three daughters-in-law locked themselves in an empty cabin and Mr Noah's three sons cowered in a corner, trapped by two fierce-looking anteaters.

Mr Noah closed his eyes for a moment.

'Why me, God?' he asked. 'I don't even like animals!'

But God was busy preparing for the mighty storm that he would send on the world and did not answer. Besides, he had every confidence in Mr Noah.

Mr Noah opened his eyes.

'Silence!' he cried in a loud voice, sounding much

braver than he felt.

To his surprise, the animals quietened down.

'Now then,' said Mr Noah. 'We're stuck in here for at least forty days and forty nights—for God said it would rain for all that time—and we must live together in a friendly fashion, sharing our food, with give and take on all sides.'

'Yeah,' muttered one of the ant-eaters. 'Give me some ants and I'll take them all right.'

'Now,' said Mr Noah, ignoring this, 'I suggest the following rules ...'

The larger of the two lions shook his magnificent mane and stepped forward.

'Pardon me,' he said, looking down his great nose. 'Pardon me, Mr Noah, but I am King of the Jungle, Lord of all Beasts, and if there's any rules to be made I make them.'

One of the tigers stood up and stretched lazily. His great claws scraped along the floor of the ark.

'Excuse me,' said the tiger in a gentle voice. 'Excuse me, but we tigers have always considered *ourselves* to be the most important of the animals, and if there's any decision-making going on round here, *we* are going to do it!'

'Fight you for it!' snapped the lion.

'As you please,' said the tiger sweetly.

Both animals bared their teeth and a minute later they

would have been at each other's throats if it had not been for Mr Noah.

'Behave yourselves!' he shouted.

Much to his surprise, the lion and tiger slunk away to opposite corners of the hall.

Feeling bolder because of his success, Mr Noah continued, 'You should be ashamed of yourselves,' he said severely. 'It's up to you both to set a good example to the other animals!'

'Now,' he said hurriedly, before the lion or tiger could answer back. 'Rule One, no fighting. Write that down, Shem. For some good reason only known to himself, God wanted two of each of you, alive, well and unharmed at the end of this voyage. And God has given me the job of looking after you. I didn't want the job, I didn't ask for it and in fact I'm beginning to think it might have been better to have drowned with everyone else than be shut up here with all of you. So if you've got any complaints, I don't want to hear them.'

There was a lot of mumbling and grumbling, squeaking and squawking, but only the tiger spoke. 'I think,' he said gravely, 'I think we should have a committee, composed of a small number of us more intelligent animals. Mr Noah can preside if he wishes.'

'What did he say?' asked one of the snakes, who was hard of hearing.

'A committee,' the tiger repeated in a louder voice, 'of

the most intelligent animals.'

'Fancies himself,' one of the geese cackled to the other. 'Those big cats are all the same.'

'Who's to say who should go on the committee?' squeaked a dormouse. 'You might be bigger than me, but are you cleverer?'

'We should *all* be on the committee,' said a giraffe, waving its long neck. 'We're all equal, aren't we? Didn't God say we're all equal?'

'*Important* was the word God used,' said Mr Noah. 'There is a difference.'

The giraffe looked as if he would disagree so Mr Noah went on hurriedly. 'But no. No committees, no discussions. We're here because God decided we should be saved.'

The mumblings and grumblings grew louder.

'Don't you *want* to be saved?' Mr Noah asked desperately.

The noise grew worse and Mr Noah and his sons escaped to the peace of their cabins and settled down to sleep.

But Mr Noah could not sleep. He lay in bed, listening to the wind howling round outside, and the snuffles and grunts of the animals inside, and he talked to God.

'Listen, God,' he said. 'It's not too late. You need a lion-tamer for this job, or a big game hunter, or at least a zoo keeper. I'm very grateful, of course, that you want to save me and my family, but honestly, I'm not cut out for the job.'

God listened to Mr Noah, but did not speak.

'And I'll tell you something, God,' Mr Noah went on. 'It's something I've never told anyone, not even my wife ... I'm scared of spiders and we've got two on board.'

God laughed, for the first time since he realized that he would have to destroy the world.

'I chose the right man for the job, Noah,' he said. 'Go to sleep now and let me worry about the animals. Oh ... and I knew about the spiders.'

And, strangely enough, Mr Noah felt comforted and fell fast asleep.

2
THE LION'S TALE

Mr Noah and his family, and two of every animal, insect and bird spent the first night safe inside the wooden ark, which God had told Mr Noah to make to save them from the flood.

But although they were safe, none of them slept well.

Mr Noah tossed and turned and had bad dreams about being drowned in the flood or eaten by an animal. Some of the animals were very noisy sleepers and kept waking him up. All night there was hissing, sighing, rumbling, muttering, squawking, squeaking, trumpeting and bellowing. It was all very disturbing.

The lion did not sleep well either. He paced angrily up and down his stall, his great tail thumping the floor behind him.

'I protest,' he said to his wife. 'I protest most strongly.'

'Mmm...?' said his wife, who was trying to sleep.

'*I* should have been put in charge of this whole operation. God should have given *me* the job. I can

15

control the animals better than Mr Noah. Aren't I the most powerful of all the beasts? Aren't I King of the Jungle?'

'Yes, dear,' said his wife sleepily. 'But we're not in the jungle now.'

The lion stopped. 'Of course we are,' he said. 'Everywhere's a jungle and only the strongest and toughest survive.' He started pacing once more, swishing his great tail from side to side. 'Only the strongest and toughest *deserve* to survive,' he added.

'Oh do be quiet and go to sleep,' his wife said. 'And

stop pacing up and down. You're making me dizzy.'

The following morning Mr Noah was just getting out of bed when there was a tap on the door of his cabin.

'Yes?' he called out sharply, in rather a bad temper because of the sleepless night. 'Who is it?'

The lion stuck his head round the door.

'I thought I ought to advise you,' he said in a majestic sort of voice, 'as you are *supposed* to be in charge here— that some of the animals are attempting to eat each other. Whether or not you can stop them is another matter. *I* could, of course, but then I'm not in charge . . .'

He found himself speaking to an empty room, for Mr Noah had run straight out of the cabin. The lion sniffed in disgust.

'Well really,' he said. 'Some people have no manners, no manners at all.' He sniffed again. 'Anyway, I'm only the messenger, a creature of no importance.'

His eye fell on the key that was in the lock of Mr Noah's cabin door and a cunning smile spread across his face.

'No importance at all,' he said in quite a different voice and padded off after Mr Noah.

In the big hall Mr Noah was horrified by what he saw.

'Stop!' he shouted. 'Stop it at once, do you hear?'

'Why should we?' asked one of the leopards.

'We always hunt for our food,' added the other.

'But you don't need to,' said Mr Noah. 'The food's all

17

provided.'

'What else are we meant to do to pass the time?' said one of the foxes.

'Well, I don't know, do I?' Mr Noah replied irritably, feeling tired, cross and rather silly when he realized he was dressed only in his nightshirt.

'Don't be such a spoilsport,' said the other fox, who was trying to coax a dormouse from its hiding place. 'It's all good fun and they *like* being hunted.'

'No, we don't,' said the dormouse, who was shivering with fright.

Mr Noah banged on the floor.

'This,' said Mr Noah loudly, 'has gone far enough! I shall make another rule: "Animals are strictly forbidden to eat one another while on this voyage." I'll get Shem to write it out and pin it up so that everyone can see.'

'But how many of us can read?' asked the monkey in a bored voice.

Mr Noah ignored this. 'I don't care what you do when we get back on dry land, but while we're in the ark you will all do as I say,' he said severely. 'Now behave yourselves while I go and get dressed.'

After he had gone the animals started muttering.

'Just who does he think he is?' asked the fox.

'God, most likely,' said the lion. He made his way through the teeming animals to the centre of the big hall. A window was set high up in the roof of the ark, and

18

through it a shaft of sunlight shone on the deep gold of the lion's mane. He looked quite magnificent.

He called in a deep voice, 'Animals—fellow travellers—friends . . . !'

'You're no friend of mine,' said the dormouse quietly.

'As I see it,' the lion went on, 'we are stuck in this ark for an unknown length of time. One of us has to be in charge and that one should be the strongest amongst us. That is the law of the jungle, as I'm sure you'll all agree.'

Some of the animals thumped their tails on the floor.

'Now this Mr Noah,' the lion continued, 'he's a good enough human, as humans go, but he isn't the strongest. So why should he be in charge?'

'Perhaps he's clever,' said one of the giraffes, frowning in concentration. 'You've got to be clever to be in charge.'

'Very true,' agreed the lion. 'And perhaps Mr Noah is clever. But it's hardly clever of him to order us about, laying down the law, making up rules as and when he chooses—now is it?'

More animals thumped their tails and there were murmurs of agreement. The lion beamed his approval.

'But,' said the dormouse timidly. 'God put Mr Noah in charge.'

The lion looked annoyed.

'*If* God did that,' he said in his grandest manner. 'Then God made a mistake.'

The tiger pricked up his ears. 'What are you up to?' he asked suspiciously.

'You'll see,' said the lion and turned and walked away.

While all this was going on in the big hall, Mr Noah was hurriedly getting dressed. As he did so, he talked to God.

'I'm not making a very good job of it, am I?' he asked humbly.

God smiled but said nothing.

'I thought,' Mr Noah went on, tying his belt round his waist, 'that if I showed them I was firm and not frightened—if I shouted a bit and laid down the law—then they'd behave properly. But I'm not sure they'll take any notice of me.'

Mr Noah put on his shoes. 'You put me in charge, God, so can't *you* do something about it? Can't you *make* them do what I say? It's for their own good.'

God sighed. 'I'm sorry, Noah. I don't rule by force.'

Noah was thinking about this when he heard a noise at the door of his cabin. He turned the handle, but the door would not open. He rattled it loudly, but the door remained firmly shut. It had been locked from the outside.

Mr Noah sat on his bed. 'What do I do, God?' he asked.

'Just wait,' said God. 'And think.'

The lion, well pleased with himself, walked back to the big hall. *That* took care of Mr Noah!

He stood in front of the crowd of animals. 'It's all sorted out,' he said. 'I'm in charge now.'

The tiger looked up. 'Who says?'

'I do,' said the lion, 'by virtue of being King of the Jungle, Lord of all Beasts, strongest...' he stopped and smiled modestly, '...and cleverest...'

'And biggest-headed,' added the monkey sourly.

'Where's Mr Noah?' asked the tiger.

'Quite safe,' said the lion. 'No need to worry—I've dealt with him.'

He smiled again and the dormouse shuddered. 'You haven't ... *eaten* him ... have you?' he asked faintly.

'Of course not,' said the lion.

'Yet,' he added.

The animals were silent.

'Now,' the lion went on briskly. 'As ruler here ...'

The tiger snarled. 'Ruler?' he said. 'You? We'll soon see about that.'

He sprang at the lion and everyone scattered as the fight began. It was a fierce fight which raged up and down and round and round the big hall, bumping off walls and flattening the smaller animals who could not get out of the way in time. The ark groaned and shook.

Mr Noah, locked in his cabin, put his head in his hands, while Mrs Noah, Shem, Ham, Japheth and their wives, who were not locked in, were all far too frightened to come out.

The other animals were frightened too, and one by one they slipped out of the big hall and made their way to Mr Noah's cabin. Eventually they were all squashed in the corridor outside.

'I don't think I want to be ruled by the lion,' said the dormouse.

'Or the tiger,' bleated one of the goats.

'Can't we ask Mr Noah to take charge again?'

suggested the dormouse.

The goat put his face to the keyhole.

'Mr Noah, we've been thinking. We'd like you to be in charge, so will you please come and stop the lion and tiger fighting.'

Mr Noah jumped off the bed and went to the door. 'Well yes,' he said. 'Of course. But I'm locked in.'

A minute later he heard the key being turned in the lock, the door opened and he was free.

Mr Noah led the procession back to the big hall. As they drew nearer the animals grew silent, listening anxiously for the sounds of fighting, but everything was quiet. Too quiet.

'Perhaps they've killed each other,' said the goat hopefully.

'Oh, I do hope not,' said Mr Noah and quickened his pace. He marched into the hall, then stopped abruptly, staring in amazement. The animals crowded round.

In front of them, side by side, lay the lion and the tiger. Worn out with fighting, they were both fast asleep and snoring gently.

The goat started to snigger, then the dormouse began squeaking and soon all the animals, insects and birds were laughing. Their laughter woke the lion and tiger.

'Wha—what happened?' asked the lion, hurriedly getting to his feet and snarling at the tiger.

'I think,' said the tiger with dignity, 'that the fight

was a draw.'

Just then the lion caught sight of Mr Noah. 'What are you doing here?' he asked. 'You should be locked in your cabin.'

The monkey pushed his way to the front, the key dangling from his long fingers. 'You might be strong,' he said, 'but you're not so clever. You left the key on the floor.'

The animals began laughing again.

'The animals came and asked me to take charge.' Mr Noah said mildly.

'Oh,' said the lion uncomfortably. 'I see.'

Mr Noah felt sorry for him. 'Look, I have an apology to make. I thought I could rule you all by shouting and laying down the law. But God doesn't rule like that and I shouldn't have tried.'

He looked at the lion. 'I'm not as strong as you, or the tiger, and I'm not very clever, but I'm very glad you locked me in because it made me talk to God and do some thinking. If we're going to survive this trip we've got to work together. So can we start again?' He put out his hand. 'Will you be my assistant, lion—and tiger, will you be my other assistant?'

There was a moment's pause before the lion said graciously. 'All right. I agree.'

'Me too,' said the tiger hurriedly.

The lion raised its great head and looked round at the

animals, who were all pressing eagerly against Mr Noah in order not to miss anything.

'Come along now,' said the lion in a grand voice. 'Give Mr Noah some room. Show some respect for the man God put in charge.'

The animals moved back and the lion left the hall in a stately fashion. Mr Noah sighed and followed. The tiger gave a crooked smile and went to his stall, while the animals, insects and birds all went to their various perching, nesting and sleeping places, and peace fell on the ark.

3

THE SHEEP'S TALE

According to God's instructions, Mr Noah, his family, and two of every animal, insect and bird were safely inside the ark well before the rain started. The rain began slowly, just a shower at first, but then the skies grew black and it began to pour. Everyone inside the ark went quiet as they listened to the sound of the rain drumming on the wooden roof. Suddenly a desperate bleating was heard above the noise.

'Mr Noah, Mr Noah . . .!'

One of the sheep ran across the big hall, its four black feet skittering this way and that on the floor, its woolly tail flopping from side to side.

'Mr Noah, something *terrible's* happened!'

'What?' asked Mr Noah.

'My wife is missing!'

'That's impossible,' said Mr Noah. 'God himself closed the door of the ark once we were all inside. And I counted you all as you came on board and there were two sheep, one ewe and one ram, just as there were two of every animal, insect and bird.'

'I know,' said the ram. 'But she isn't in the ark now, I've looked everywhere.'

Mr Noah thought for a moment, then he turned to the lion and tiger. 'She can't have gone far because the ark isn't *that* large,' he said. 'Will you help me search?'

'Of course,' said the lion graciously. 'Although,' he added in a low voice, 'why anyone would want to bother with a sheep is beyond me.'

'Unless you were hungry,' muttered the tiger, with a flash of his gleaming teeth.

The animals searched the ark from end to end and from top to bottom but there was no sign of the missing sheep.

'Oh dear,' said Mr Noah. 'I must talk to God about this.'

So he went to his cabin and shut the door.

While Mr Noah was talking to God, the missing sheep was outside, standing under a tree on the top of a rocky mountain, trying, unsuccessfully, to shelter from the rain. As the rain splashed through the branches, she though that perhaps she should not have been in such a hurry to leave the ark in the first place, and that perhaps the ark was not so bad after all. At least it was dry.

When all the animals had arrived at the ark, she had followed the ram up the ramp and waited patiently while

Mr Noah hunted through his long list.

'Sheep. Now let me see... seagulls... snails—no, before snails—ah yes, "Sheep, two, one ewe, one ram".' He ticked them off his list and they had entered the ark.

The ewe had looked in amazement at the massive wooden building. She had wandered from deck to deck, searching for something familiar, a patch of fresh green grass, a tree. But there was no green grass in the ark and there were no trees. There was food, yes, stored in great wooden containers, enough for all the animals, but nothing comfortable to lie on except some dry straw, nothing comfortable to chew on, and nothing at all to look at.

'Why have we come?' she asked the ram.

'Because Mr Noah told us to,' he replied. 'So that we could be saved from the flood.'

'I'm not sure I believe in this flood,' she said. 'I can't really believe that *all* the earth will be covered with

water, can you?'

It was one of the great eagles who answered her. He was sitting on a wooden beam high above the big hall.

'I'm afraid, madam, I do believe in it,' he said sadly. 'And although I wouldn't say this in Mr Noah's hearing, for he's a good man, between you and me I think it's a bit hard on all the animals and birds who have been left behind to drown in the flood. It's not our fault that the earth needs destroying—it's the fault of humans, not us.'

He flew off to the upper deck—for eagles like to be as high as possible—leaving the ewe and the ram in the hall.

'It still seems a lot of nonsense to me,' said the ewe. 'After all, we've only Mr Noah's word that this flood is going to happen.'

She left her partner and returned to the entrance to watch as more and more animals, insects and birds arrived.

'Hmm,' she thought to herself. 'It's going to be very crowded in here when everyone's aboard.'

There was already a terrible noise in the ark as the new arrivals chattered, squeaked, grunted and howled as they made themselves at home.

29

She looked past Mr Noah to the clearing in the forest where the ark had been built. Beyond the trees lay the gentle curve of a hill, thick with green grass and dappled with sunlight.

As Mr Noah was busy welcoming more animals, the sheep slipped quietly away from the ark and no one saw her go. She scampered through the forest until she reached the hill, then she wandered along, grazing contentedly. The grass, deep and thick and delicious, seemed to go on for ever. It was springy beneath her feet. The sky was blue, birds flashed and darted overhead and insects hummed and buzzed drowsily.

For six days she wandered, scarcely noticing the clouds that drifted across the sky, small wisps at first, then growing and thickening until at last the sun was blotted out.

When the first drops of rain fell, the sheep did not mind too much because she had a fine coat of wool to protect her. It was only when her coat was wet through that she began to shiver. She ran to a tree for shelter.

'I can stay here until the rain stops and then dry my coat in the sun,' she thought.

But the rain did not stop and the sun did not come out. The great round drops fell faster and faster and the clouds grew so thick and black they seemed to reach right down to the earth.

'Perhaps it was true what the eagle said,' the sheep

thought. 'Perhaps I should have stayed in the ark, but how was I to know that Mr Noah would be right?' She sighed. 'I'll just have to find my own way back and hope they'll take me in.'

But by now everything was hidden in a great blanket of mist. The sheep had no idea where the ark was or even where she was and she was suddenly very, very frightened. She walked round and round and up and down. The path began to climb, growing steeper and steeper, and as she struggled along it, the sheep knew that she was completely lost. And still it rained, and rained, and rained.

Inside the ark, Mr Noah was talking to God.

'These animals in the ark are my responsibility, God, so I must go and rescue her. But how?' He paused. 'I can't

swim, you see. At least, not very well.'

God smiled. 'Why don't you ask the animals?' he said.

Mr Noah nodded. 'Yes. I will.' He got up to go. 'Oh, and until we can rescue the sheep, will you look after her?'

'Of course,' said God.

'Yes,' said Mr Noah. 'Silly of me to have asked.'

He left his cabin, went to the big hall and called all the animals together.

'One of the sheep is missing,' he said, 'and I must go and find her.'

'How?' asked the monkey bluntly.

'Well,' said Mr Noah. 'I shall leave the ark and look for her.' He went to the big door and gave it a push. But it would not open from the inside for God had shut it tight.

'Trapped!' screeched the emu. 'We're trapped!'

The animals were silent. Suddenly the ark creaked and shuddered from end to end.

'We're afloat,' said the monkey.

'I don't like it,' said the ostrich, trying, unsuccessfully, to bury his head in the wooden planks of the floor.

'I never was good on boats,' said the dog, turning pale. 'Suffer from seasickness something horrid.'

'Please,' said Mr Noah. 'Let me think.'

'Let's *all* think,' said the lion.

'Couldn't we build a boat?' asked the beaver.

'*This* is a boat,' said the monkey scornfully.

'Yes, but if we made a small boat, we could row it and

steer it where we wanted. We can't steer the ark.'

'And what do you suggest we make it with?' asked the monkey sarcastically. 'Chop up the ark for wood?'

The beaver was silent.

'I think we should leave that silly sheep behind,' hissed the snake.

'So do I,' agreed the emu. 'She had no right to go and leave the ark. It's her own fault.'

Several of the animals agreed.

'It's not right to put the rest of us in danger,' added the snake. You must think of us, Mr Noah.'

The ram stood up. 'Look, I understand what you are all feeling and I know my wife was silly to go off like that, but she *is* my wife and I love her and I don't want to stay on this ark without her.' He turned to Mr Noah. 'If no one is prepared to rescue her then please let me go and be with her. She must be so frightened.'

'Of course we'll rescue her,' said Mr Noah. 'Each one of you is important, God said so. He also put me in charge, so it's my duty to go and find her. If I can't get out by the door, I shall have to jump from the roof. If I don't come back, Shem, you will take over charge here under God.'

He walked to the ladder leading to the trapdoor in the roof of the ark. 'Pity I never learnt to swim properly,' he muttered to himself under his breath. The eagle, who had very good hearing, called down to him.

'Mr Noah! Wait!' He flew to the ground. 'If it was left to me, I'd say we should leave the sheep behind, but if you say she's got to be rescued then I'll do it. You'll only drown.'

Mr Noah looked at the eagle with its fierce eyes and cruel beak. 'Are you sure?' he asked doubtfully.

'Of course I am,' said the eagle. He looked at Mr Noah. 'And don't worry. I promise I won't hurt her, although she deserves it.'

Mr Noah thanked the great eagle and pushed open the trapdoor. The eagle flew up and perched on the edge. He looked round at the driving rain, the grey swirling waters and the white mist.

'How very sad,' he said.

'What can you see?' Mr Noah asked anxiously.

'Very little,' said the eagle. 'The water is rising fast and the mist is thick. But wait . . .'

He stretched his great wings and soared off into the sky. With his keen eyesight he had seen the topmost peak of a mountain which jutted out of the waters of the flood, looking like a tiny island in a swelling and fast-rising sea. At the very top, clinging forlornly to a rock, under a tree, was the missing sheep, wet, trembling and very scared.

The eagle swooped down out of the mist. He caught hold of her woolly coat in his great talons, lifted her up and flew back with her across the angry waters. His wings hurt with the effort, his eyes were almost blinded by the rain, but at last he reached the ark.

Mr Noah opened the trapdoor from inside, caught the sheep in his arms and brought her to safety inside the ark.

'I'm sorry,' said the sheep.

'That's all right,' said Mr Noah. 'I'm just glad you're home.'

He looked at the wet, shivering eagle. 'Thank you,' he said.

'Think nothing of it,' said the eagle, and promptly went to sleep.

4

THE TERMITE'S TALE

The rain, once started, did not stop, and soon the ark, containing Mr Noah, his family, and two of every kind of animal, insect and bird, was floating on top of the water which covered the earth.

Outside it was wet, but inside the ark was dry and snug and warm, if not entirely comfortable. It was not very comfortable to be living inside a wooden ark containing two of every living creature made by God—apart, of course, from fish.

'But it's better than being drowned in the flood,' Mr Noah told his wife, and she agreed.

There was a scratching at the door of Mr Noah's cabin and the lion came in.

'Excuse me, Mr Noah, but I think you ought to come. We've a slight problem,' he said. 'Well, a number of problems, in fact,' he added.

Mr Noah, who had been enjoying a quiet rest before feeding the animals, got wearily to his feet and followed

the lion to the upper deck.

As he climbed the steps he could hear a faint plopping noise which grew louder as he reached the top. When he turned the corner he could see drops of water falling onto the floor.

'It's not the only leak,' said the lion gloomily. 'The tiger and I have counted four already.'

'Oh dear,' said Mr Noah. He stared at the puddle on the floor. 'What are we going to do?'

One or two of the animals had followed them.

'*We* aren't going to do anything,' said the monkey in a smug voice. '*You* built the ark—*you* solve the problem.'

Mr Noah looked worried. 'I know my carpentry isn't very good, but God told me that the ark was watertight when we set off.' He called his sons. 'Shem, Ham, Japheth—do we have any bits of wood left over— anything we can use to fill the gaps?'

His sons shook their heads. 'We used it all on the building,' Shem said.

'And we didn't bring anything for repairs,' added Ham.

'Stupid of me not to think of that,' said Mr Noah. 'Right,' he went on in a brisk voice. 'The first thing is to catch the drips.'

Soon a bowl was placed under each hole. When they were full of water, they were emptied out of the trapdoor at the top of the ark.

But after a day or two *more* holes began to appear.

Mr Noah called a meeting of all the animals and asked for their help.

The elephants obligingly placed their long trunks up against two of the holes and sucked in as much water as they could before blowing it out of the trapdoor.

The giraffes stretched their long necks and stopped two more of the holes by wedging their heads against them. But they soon developed headaches and neckaches and had to stop.

The peacock, after much grumbling, spread his beautiful tail over one of the holes like an umbrella. The beavers offered to dam the holes if any mud and stones could be found. But nothing worked for long.

The ark began to feel decidedly damp and the only animals happy with the situation were the two hippopotami, who had missed the lakes of their home and stood for hours under the holes, wallowing under the steady drops of water.

Mr Noah had a talk with God.

'I'm sorry to trouble you, God, especially with all the problems you have with the flood and everything, but we've got problems here and I don't know what to do about it.'

'Tell me,' said God, although of course he already knew.

'You did say that the ark was watertight, and of

course I believe you, but it's not watertight now. It's sprung a leak—well, a lot of leaks actually—and some of them are more than leaks, they're downright holes and we're finding it very difficult to catch all the water. Perhaps my carpentry was worse than I thought,' Mr Noah added miserably.

'There was nothing wrong with your work, Noah,' God assured him. 'The ark was quite watertight when you set out. Keep your eyes and ears open and you will soon find the cause of the trouble.'

That night, when all the animals were asleep, Mr Noah was woken by a strange noise. He had grown used to the grunts and snores, the whistles and murmurings of the animals and could sleep through them, but this was different. He lay in his cabin and listened.

'Tap ... tap, tap ... tap ...'

It stopped but soon started again further away. Mr Noah got up and left his cabin. Walking on bare feet he silently made his way towards the sound, pausing now and again to listen. The tapping grew louder. Mr Noah climbed the steps, from the bottom deck, to the middle, to the top. He crept along the corridor and the tapping grew louder still. He turned a corner ...

... and stumbled across two woodpeckers, who were busy tapping into the wood with their long beaks and hard heads.

'Just a minute!' said Mr Noah, in a loud voice.

The woodpeckers turned and a fine spray of water began to dribble in through the holes they had just made.

'Hello, Mr Noah,' said one of the woodpeckers.

'What do you think you're doing?' Mr Noah asked sternly.

'It's obvious,' said the other woodpecker. 'We're pecking wood.'

'It's what we always do,' said the first woodpecker kindly. 'Peck wood.'

'That's why we're called...'

'WOODPECKERS!' they both shouted together and flew about laughing.

'But don't you know what will happen if you keep pecking?' Mr Noah asked. 'If you go on this way, we could sink.'

'No, we won't,' said the second woodpecker cheerfully.

'God'll save us, you'll see,' said the first with confidence.

'I'm sorry, but you can't go on doing it,' Mr Noah said in a decided voice. The woodpeckers looked upset.

'But we've got to peck something,' the first one said.

'It's in our nature, see,' the second one added.

'We make these holes to live in,' explained the first. 'But we can't live in any of the holes we've made here.'

'They're too wet,' the second one added disapprovingly.

'But we've provided holes for you to live in,' said Mr
Noah.

The second woodpecker sniffed. 'It's not the same.'

The first woodpecker flapped his wings. 'And anyway, we *like* pecking wood. That's why we're called . . .'

'All right, all right,' said Mr Noah hastily. 'Just give
me time to think about it.' He could not think properly
with wet, cold feet. 'Just promise to stop for now.'

'Okay,' said the first woodpecker. 'We were going to
pack it in for tonight anyway.'

Mr Noah spent the rest of the night deep in thought

and in the morning he had an answer. He went to the woodpeckers.

'How would you feel if I let you peck at a harmless piece of wood, perhaps the door to a cabin? Would that keep you happy?'

The woodpeckers considered.

'Well—so long as it's good wood,' said the first warily.

'All the wood on this ark is good,' said Mr Noah with dignity. 'God chose it himself.'

The woodpeckers pondered.

'All right,' said the first. 'It's a deal.'

So everyone was happy, apart from Shem, whose cabin door was chosen by the woodpeckers and whose days and nights were, from then on, rather noisy.

But there still remained the problem of the leaks in the ark. It was raining harder than ever now and more and more water was coming in.

'What are we going to do, God?' Mr Noah asked, quite worn out with baling out the water.

'Have you asked the animals for their ideas?' God said.

'Of course,' said Mr Noah. 'Everyone's helping. The elephants are holding their trunks . . .'

'Yes,' said God. 'I know that. But have you asked *everyone*?'

'Yes,' said Mr Noah confidently. 'Everyone. At least,' he added doubtfully. 'I think I have.'

So Mr Noah walked round the ark, speaking to large animals and small, to wild animals and tame, to insects and birds—but no one had any suggestions on how to fill the holes. Just as he was about to give up he caught sight of a strange black mound in a dark corner of the ark. He stopped, looked, then tapped politely. Two white, wriggling ant-like creatures came out.

'Yes?' one of them asked.

'Excuse me, but who are you?' asked Mr Noah.

'Well, really!' said the other. 'You should know, Mr Noah—you ticked us off your list!'

'Did I?' said Mr Noah. 'I'm terribly sorry but there were so many, I've forgotten. Are you ants?'

'Ants indeed!' said the first huffily. 'We're *termites*! Quite different!'

'We are distantly related,' said the other termite mildly. 'Somewhere along the family tree.'

'*Very* distantly,' said the first.

'Well, I'm sorry,' Mr Noah said again. He touched the hard black mound. 'Would you mind telling me what this is?'

'It's our home,' said the first termite.

'You made it?' Mr Noah asked.

'Yes, of course!'

'What of?'

'Wood.'

Mr Noah was puzzled. 'But you haven't used any of

44

the wood on the ark—have you?' he asked.

'No. We've used our own.'

Mr Noah was even more puzzled. 'Your *own*?'

'It's quite simple really,' said the second termite. 'We feed on wood and store it inside our bodies. When we want to build a home, we just use it as we want. When we knew we were coming on this trip we stored a lot of wood as we didn't know what the living conditions would be like on the ark.'

'Besides,' added the first, 'we like to live in our own nest.'

Mr Noah tapped the termite house. 'And is it strong?' he asked.

'Strong!' echoed the first termite. 'I'll tell you something, Mr Noah. This nest is a lot stronger than your ark.'

'Would you—could you—please—give us some help then?' Mr Noah asked anxiously. 'We're in a dreadful pickle and I think you are the only ones who can get us out.'

The termites agreed so Mr Noah went away to organize the animals. The woodpeckers pecked away at Shem's cabin door and the beavers collected the wood shavings and took them to the termites. The termites ate the wood and produced the hard black substance they used in making their homes. The elephants, using their trunks, plastered the holes with the mixture and the peacock waved his tail to help dry it quickly.

One by one the holes were sealed and the bowls returned to their proper uses. Everyone on the ark was soon dry and comfortable again—as comfortable as it was possible to be with two of every animal, insect and bird living so close to one another, not to mention Mr Noah, Mrs Noah, their three sons and their wives.

And the ark did not sink but continued to float on the troubled waters of the world as the rain fell without stopping, day after day after day.

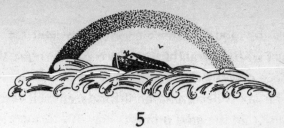

5

THE SKUNK'S TALE

Mr Noah, his family and two of every insect, animal and bird began to settle into their new life inside the ark, while the rain which God had sent flooded the earth.

Mr Noah was kept very busy each day settling arguments, looking after sick animals and generally trying to keep his little world as happy and content as possible. Each evening he went round the ark to make sure that everyone was comfortable for the night.

One evening, as he climbed to the second deck, he heard angry voices.

'Animals like you shouldn't be allowed!'

Mr Noah hurried up the steps.

'Disgraceful!'

'Anti-social!'

'Throw them overboard, I say!'

Mr Noah sniffed, then sniffed again, wrinkling his nose at the nasty smell which drifted down the corridor. He saw a group of animals huddled together and, as their voices grew louder, the smell grew stronger.

'Just who do you think you are, going round stinking the place out?' bleated the goat.

'This ark is becoming unfit for decent self-respecting animals,' said the emu primly.

'And insects,' added the ant.

'And birds,' said the vulture. 'We vultures have very sensitive noses.'

A burst of really smelly air made the animals fall back and Mr Noah could see two black and white spotted skunks, their backs to the wall.

The emu, overcome by the smell, fell flat on the floor, right on top of the hedgehog. 'Ow...! The pain! The smell!'

'Sorry, I'm sure,' said the hedgehog politely, struggling to get out from under her.

The skunks said nothing. They stood on their front legs, bared their sharp teeth and stamped up and down on the ground. Then they fell on all fours, lifted their tails and squirted some more smell at the animals, who began to creep away.

The goat trotted over to Mr Noah.

'Did you see that?' he asked.

'Yes,' said Mr Noah. 'And smelt it.'

'It's not right,' said the emu feebly. 'It shouldn't be allowed.'

The goose waved its long thin neck at Mr Noah.

'What are you going to do about it?' she asked.

'I think,' said Mr Noah, 'we'd better have a talk.'

They met, a short time later, in the big hall. All the animals were there—apart from the two skunks—and feelings ran high. The goat stopped Mr Noah as soon as he entered.

'That smell is making this place extremely unpleasant,' he complained.

'I didn't know it was going to be like this,' said the snail, 'or I wouldn't have come.'

'Please, everyone,' said Mr Noah. 'Can't we solve this in a friendly way? We all have habits that others don't like, but we've got to get along together. Can't you learn to live with the smell?'

'No,' said the fox bluntly.

'In my opinion, for what it's worth,' said the camel in a slow, deliberate voice, 'I think the skunks should be told in no uncertain terms that we are not prepared to tolerate their anti-social behaviour and if they don't immediately cease fouling the air we shall have no alternative but to remove them straightaway from this ... from this ...' he peered around ' ... edifice.'

'What's he talking about?' asked the giraffe.

'If they don't stop smelling we'll throw them out,' said the fox bluntly.

The lion looked at Mr Noah. 'If you want my advice—speaking as your assistant of course—unless something is done soon there'll be a riot.'

'Very well,' said Mr Noah, 'I'll see what I can do.'

Mr Noah returned to the skunks. But as he approached, they stood up and glared.

Mr Noah spoke very quickly. 'Look,' he said. 'Friends. I'm sorry to have to say this, but you've upset all the animals—to say nothing of the insects and birds—and they are not at all happy.'

The skunks rose on their front legs. Mr Noah, his own legs feeling weak and trembly, took a step backwards.

'In the interests of good relations you'll have to stop smelling the place out, otherwise we shall have to take stern action.'

The skunks stamped vigorously on the floor, stared him straight in the face and shot out a horrible smell. Mr Noah fell to the ground and banged his head with such force that he was knocked unconscious.

He came round to find himself in his cabin. He felt his sore head gently.

'What should I do, God?' he asked.

'You could try talking to them,' said God.

'I've just tried,' Mr Noah said indignantly, 'and look where it got me!'

'You didn't talk *to* them, you talked *at* them,' said God patiently.

'*You* talk to them then,' Mr Noah said grumpily. 'They might listen to you. At least *you* won't end up with a sore head.'

God laughed.

'It's no laughing matter,' said Mr Noah severely. 'I've a crisis on my hands and you're supposed to help.'

He really was feeling rather ill, otherwise he would not have spoken to God like that.

'I *am* helping, Noah,' God said gently. 'I'm giving you advice. Talk *to* the skunks and find out what is wrong.'

But Mr Noah did not want to take God's advice. He lay in his bed and nursed his sore head while the smell continued to spread right through the ark. One by one the animals, insects and birds came to his cabin to complain. Mr Noah pretended that his head was worse than it really was and refused to get up. But at last the smell grew so bad that Mr Noah had to do something. He sent for the lion and the tiger.

'Lion,' he said in a weak voice. 'And tiger. My

assistants. You know I'm laid up here with a broken head and so I can't do anything about the smell. But something must be done.'

'The animals are very angry,' said the lion. 'They might even take matters into their own hands.'

'You mean . . .?'

'Wring their smelly necks,' said the tiger.

Mr Noah was shocked. 'Lion . . . tiger . . . would you . . . could you . . . talk to the skunks on my behalf?'

'No,' said the tiger bluntly.

'They'd listen to you,' pleaded Mr Noah, 'animals like themselves.'

'But *you* have the authority,' said the lion gently. 'Authority from God. Far be it from me, a mere lion, to take over that authority.' He looked at Mr Noah and opened his eyes wide. 'Who knows where it could end? Why—the animals might even want me—us,' he added hastily as the tiger growled, 'to take over command here.'

'Yes,' said Mr Noah, 'Well—of course—I fully intend to deal with this, just as soon as I've recovered.'

The lion smiled sweetly. 'I wouldn't leave it too long,' he said, and he and the tiger left.

Mr Noah then sent for his eldest son.

'Shem,' he said. 'I've an important job for you.'

'Yes, Father?'

'I want you to try to find out why the skunks give off that terrible smell and persuade them, if you can, to stop.'

Shem turned pale. 'Me, Father?'

'Yes, you.'

'Very well, Father.'

Shem went out of the cabin but returned after only a few moments, looking dazed and sick.

'I did try, Father, I really did, but I just couldn't get near them.'

'All right, all right,' said Mr Noah testily. 'Send Ham to me.'

When Ham came Mr Noah gave him the same instructions. Ham turned green.

'Me, Father? You want me to go?'

'Yes,' said Mr Noah.

'But I suffer from sea-sickness. That smell will make me very, very ill.'

'Just do as I say,' said Mr Noah.

So Ham went out of the cabin but he was back even faster than his brother.

'Sorry, Dad.'

'You didn't even try,' grumbled Mr Noah. 'Send Japheth to me. He's a good, obedient lad.'

But Japheth was so frightened at the thought of having to deal with the skunks that he sent a note saying that he was too unwell even to leave his cabin. Mr Noah lay back in bed.

'Noah.'

It was God.

'Noah, I did not save you and your family from the flood or put you in charge of all the animals, insects and birds left in the world for you to disobey me.'

'Me, Lord?'

'Yes. I told *you* to talk to the skunks, not the lion or the tiger or your sons.'

'I thought I was just dealing with the matter as best I could,' said Mr Noah weakly. 'While I'm not well.'

'You thought nothing of the sort,' said God. 'Come on, Noah. Get up.'

'You're not ... angry ... with me?' Mr Noah asked anxiously.

'No,' said God. 'Just a little sad.'

Mr Noah felt ashamed. 'I'm sorry, God,' he said. .

He got up, dressed, and went to see the skunks. The smell, by now, was frightful, and Mr Noah held his breath as he climbed the steps. The skunks were in their usual place, surrounded, at a safe distance, by a circle of threatening animals.

'Going to throw them overboard?' asked the fox.

'If you don't, I'll gladly tear out their throats,' said the leopard, pacing up and down. 'That'll soon stop their smell.'

'Just give me a minute with them,' said Mr Noah. 'Alone.'

The animals were surprised but did as he said and moved away. Mr Noah held out his hand.

'Come,' he said, 'I'm not going to threaten or harm you.'

The skunks rose to their feet and Mr Noah swallowed nervously.

'I just want you to tell me why you are making such a smell,' he said in a quavering voice.

One of the skunks stamped.

'Please,' said Mr Noah. 'I'm sorry if I frightened you before. I was just scared. I'm scared now.'

'Scared?' said one of the skunks. 'You? That's a laugh!'

The other skunk hissed. 'Shut up, you fool, it's all a

plot.' She turned to Mr Noah and squirted the foul smell at him, but Mr Noah ducked and missed its full force.

'I don't care what you do,' he said, feeling quite sick. 'I don't care if you knock me unconscious again. I only want to help you.'

The skunk got ready to squirt Mr Noah again, but the first one stopped her.

'Hold on a moment.' He turned to Mr Noah. 'You want to know why we make this smell, right?'

'Right,' said Mr Noah.

'Wouldn't you make a smell if you were scared witless?' the skunk said bluntly.

'But why are you scared?' asked Mr Noah.

'Wouldn't you be, if you were threatened by a load of animals, most of them bigger than you?'

'Why *did* they threaten you?'

'It was that goose started it,' said the other skunk sulkily. 'Flapping around, accusing us of pushing her. And then it went from bad to worse with all of them shouting and saying they'd do all sorts of horrible things to us. No wonder we smelt.'

'We were scared, see, and when we're scared we give off a smell,' explained the first skunk. 'Works wonderfully most times.'

'I see,' said Mr Noah. 'Well, look, God put me in charge here, although I don't know why because I'm not making a very good job of it. If I told you that you've nothing at all to be frightened about, would you believe me?'

'So long as the rest of the animals stop scaring us,' said the skunk.

'Come with me,' said Mr Noah.

He led the skunks to the big hall and they stood, rather uncomfortably, beside him while he explained to the animals, insects and birds that the skunks had only given off the smell because they had been frightened. After some discussion, the animals agreed not to frighten the skunks any more so long as the skunks stopped smelling. In fact, some of the smaller animals, who knew what it was like to feel scared, went out of their way to make the skunks feel safe and at home.

So the skunks became part of the family of the ark and the little world of the ark floated on and on.

6

THE DONKEY'S TALE

When God sent a great flood to destroy the earth, he told Mr Noah to make a wooden ark and take inside it his own family and two of every living creature in order to keep them alive. Two of every animal, insect and bird were living in the ark and it was full to bursting.

As many of the animals, insects and birds had never even seen, let alone lived with, other animals, insects and birds, there was much fighting and arguing before they all settled down together reasonably happily.

When the donkey arrived on board he was amazed at all the different creatures. On that first day, while his wife went to the stall given to them for the journey, he walked slowly round the big hall, wondering at everything he saw.

'I've never seen anything like it,' he said to his wife when at last he joined her. 'Did you know, my dear, that there's an incredible beast—well, two of them, of course—with huge long noses, so long that they touch the ground? They are very big and very heavy and I believe that Mr Noah is worried about them sharing accommodation, in case they overbalance the ark.'

'I expect you mean the elephants, dear,' said his wife, who prided herself upon her general knowledge.

'I expect I do,' agreed the donkey. He went off again, but soon returned.

'There's another animal,' he said excitedly, 'a great tall thing, with a long, long neck and a small head at the top.'

'A giraffe,' said his wife.

'If you say so,' said the donkey. He went off once more, but was soon trotting back.

'Did you know that there's an animal that can run as fast as the wind?' he said in wonder. 'He's running round the big hall now to keep himself in training.'

'Oh, a cheetah,' said his wife, not really very interested.

'And there's another animal with the most powerful hind legs. I was told that he can jump huge distances. I've never seen such an odd-shaped creature before.'

'Well, dear,' said his wife, 'kangaroos live in a different part of the world from us, so it's not surprising that we've never seen them.'

The donkey left the cabin and did not return until it was dark.

'There's an animal,' he said, breathlessly, 'that gives off light. It glows. It's called a glow-worm,' he added hurriedly, before his wife could speak.

'That's not an animal, that's an insect,' his wife said.

'Yes, dear,' said the donkey humbly. He looked at her in astonishment. 'How do you know so much?' he asked.

'I've kept my eyes and my ears open,' she said placidly.

'Don't you want to come and look at all the wonderful creatures in the hall?' asked the donkey.

'Later, dear,' she said. 'Right now, it's nice not to be working and I'm enjoying the holiday.'

So the donkey wandered round the ark on his own and marvelled and wondered at the variety of all the creatures God had made. But as the days passed, his wonder turned to envy. He looked down at himself and sighed.

'There are some beautiful animals in the ark,' he said. 'They make my old grey coat look very dull and boring.'

'Never mind,' said his wife affectionately. 'I like you just as you are.'

But the donkey was not consoled.

'Why are we so drab?' he asked.

'That's how God made us,' she replied.

'Well, I don't think it's fair,' said the donkey. 'Our life is boring enough as it is. Why couldn't God have made us beautiful? Why couldn't we have had something to be proud of—a beautiful tail, perhaps, like the peacock?'

'The peacock's *wife* has a very boring tail,' said his wife dryly, but the donkey was not listening.

'What are we, anyway? Just beasts of burden, only fit to fetch and carry,' he said gloomily. 'Tied up when we're not working and beaten if we don't work hard enough.'

'Someone has to do the work,' said his wife practically. 'We can't all be beautiful or clever. Anyway, we can't change what we are so we'd better make the best of it.'

But the donkey could not do that. Perhaps, he thought to himself, he *could* change if he tried hard enough. But he did not tell this to his wife. So he watched the elephant with his long trunk and tried pulling his own nose in the hope that it would grow. All he got was a sore nose.

He tried craning his neck, hoping it would lengthen

and become interesting like the giraffe's, but all he got was a stiff neck.

He practised jumping and challenged the kangaroo to a jumping match. He lost.

He tried running, but could only manage a fast trot and was soon tired out.

The other animals soon realized what he was doing. Some of them laughed but others were more sympathetic.

'Poor old donkey, trying to change into something more interesting,' said the elephant.

'Like me,' said the peacock, spreading his lovely tail.

'Someone ought to tell him it's no use,' the elephant went on.

'I really don't know why he bothers,' said the goat.

'If I looked as dull as he does, I'd bother,' said the leopard, who was very proud of his spots.

'He's only making an ass of himself,' said the fox and doubled up with laughter at his joke. 'He'll probably start to jump off tables, thinking that he can fly,' he said when he had finished laughing.

After a few days the donkey began to despair of ever changing into something less dull and boring. But one day he saw an animal he had not seen before. It looked rather like him in its shape and size but its coat was very different, for it was striped all over with great black and white stripes. The donkey was entranced.

'Excuse me,' he asked timidly. 'But—who are you?'

'Me?' said the animal, tossing its head. 'A zebra. And you're a donkey.'

'Yes,' admitted the donkey, ashamed. 'Please... can you tell me... how did you get those amazing, those wonderful stripes?'

'I was born with them,' the zebra replied.

'Oh,' said the donkey sadly.

'Don't tell me,' said his wife when he returned to his stall. 'You've met the zebra.'

'How did you know?' asked the donkey.

'I guessed. It had to happen some time or other.'

The donkey sighed and wandered off, thinking hard. How to get stripes—how, *how* to get those wonderful, bold, black and white stripes? He spent the whole day thinking. He kept apart from the other animals and missed all his meals. When night fell and the animals had settled down to sleep the donkey had got no further in his thinking. Suddenly he realized that he was very, very hungry.

The donkey trotted off to find the food stores. He lost his way and ended up in the kitchen used by Mr and Mrs Noah to prepare food for themselves and their family. There was nobody around.

He was about to leave when he saw a large bowl filled to the brim with something that looked like food. The donkey trotted over to it and snuffed his nose over the

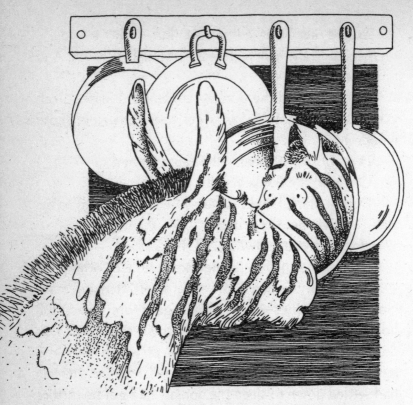

edge. The bowl spun off the table and on to the floor and
the donkey was covered with a fine powdering of flour.
He stepped back in alarm and his bottom collided with a
pan of water, which splashed over him. Quite frightened
by now, the donkey turned to go... and there, facing
him, was the zebra.

'I'm so sorry,' the donkey said apologetically. 'I didn't
know this was your place. I'll get out right away.'

The zebra did not answer. It just looked at him with

big frightened eyes while water ran off its back and dripped slowly onto the floor. The donkey realized that he was staring at himself, his face reflected in the shiny surface of one of the pans.

He stared and stared and could not believe his eyes. 'It's me,' he said at last. 'And I'm striped.' He looked down at his legs. 'I've become a zebra. It's . . . it's a miracle.'

As if in a dream the donkey went out of the kitchen and into the big hall. The monkey, disturbed by the clatter, opened an eye as he passed.

'Oh, so it was you, was it, making that row just now?' he said sourly. 'Can't you let a poor animal sleep?' He opened the other eye and stared in amazement.

'Well, now I've seen everything,' he said.

The guinea-pig, who was a light sleeper, squinted up at the donkey and began to giggle. The owl swooped down to get a better look and in no time at all, all the animals, insects and birds were awake and staring at the donkey. They stared, then they laughed . . . and laughed . . . and laughed.

'That's the funniest thing I've ever seen,' said the crocodile, holding on to his scaly sides with his claws.

The donkey looked round, puzzled. Why were they all laughing? Why weren't they admiring him in his new zebra coat?

At last the noise woke his wife and she came into the big hall. When she saw him she shook her head. 'You silly old thing,' she said fondly.

'Why?' asked the donkey, bewildered. 'What have I done?'

The fresh wave of laughter brought Mr Noah hurrying into the hall. He stopped still in amazement when he saw the donkey, but he did not laugh. He was not even angry when he realized that the flour for the next day's bread was plastered all over the donkey's back.

'Come along, old thing,' he said. 'Let's clean you off, shall we?'

He led the bewildered donkey away and washed all traces of flour from his coat. It took a long time because the flour and water had mixed to form a hard paste. He spoke gently to the donkey, but the donkey just stood with his head bowed and did not say a word. As soon as he was clean he trotted slowly away.

'He'll soon get over it,' Mr Noah said to himself.

But the donkey did not get over it. He stopped talking to his wife, he stopped walking around the big hall, he stopped trying to change into something different, he even stopped eating. He just lay in the corner of his stall, growing weaker and weaker.

At last his wife went to see Mr Noah.

'Can't you do something, Mr Noah?' she asked. 'I've tried talking to him. Some of the animals have come to see him to say they are sorry they laughed, but nothing works. I'm really worried. If he doesn't eat, he'll die.'

When she had gone, Mr Noah talked to God.

'How can I help the donkey, God?' he asked. 'His wife and the animals have all tried.'

God thought for a moment, then said: 'Go to the donkey and tell him this. Tell him that ordinary, every-day creatures are very dear to me. Tell him that those who are beaten, mocked and laughed at by others have a place close to my heart. And so has he. Tell him that although others think he's a fool and he thinks he's dull and boring, he will prove wiser than many men. And tell him this—that one day a donkey, like himself, will bear my Son upon his back and ride proudly through a great city, and people will cheer him and throw fresh leaves and flowers in his path. Comfort him with my words—for he is very special to me.'

So Mr Noah went to the donkey and told him everything that God had said. At first the donkey would not listen. But in a little while he got to his feet and began to take some food. And when at last he was persuaded by Mr Noah and his wife to go into the big hall, he met with great kindness from the other animals, and nobody laughed at him, so that he soon felt quite well and happy.

'Perhaps it's not such a bad thing to be a donkey,' he said that night to his wife. 'Not if we're special to God.'

7

THE SON'S TALE

When God told Mr Noah to build the ark which was to save him and two of every animal, insect and bird in the world from the flood, God also told Mr Noah to take his wife, his three sons, Shem, Ham and Japheth and their wives into the ark so that they, too, would be saved.

The three sons helped their father build the ark, using wood specially chosen by God, and when the animals, insects and birds began to arrive, Shem, Ham and Japheth were there beside Mr Noah, sorting out problems, showing the animals where to sleep and looking after the hundred and one things that needed doing before everyone was safely inside.

They all took turns in cooking, cleaning and keeping the ark in good condition during the voyage. There was a lot of work to be done and, to begin with, no one grumbled. They were all much too grateful to be alive as the rain began to fall and the earth disappeared under the waters of the flood.

It was crowded on the ark and, after a while, tempers began to grow short. The rain fell steadily, day after day. Ham, especially, found life difficult.

'I'm bored,' he said one day to his elder brother.

Shem was surprised. 'I don't know how you can be bored with all this work,' he said.

'Well, I am,' said Ham. 'And I'm fed up. We shouldn't be doing work like this, cleaning up after the animals, feeding the animals, watering the animals, making sure they're kept happy.'

'Well, if we don't keep the animals happy, there's no hope for any of us,' Shem said.

'Nobody worries if *I'm* happy,' Ham said as he left the cabin.

Outside the cabin he stumbled over the hedgehog.

'Can't you look where you're going?' he asked angrily.

'I could say the same to you,' replied the hedgehog mildly, 'but I won't. Good day to you.'

Soon after that, the lion went to see Mr Noah.

'Acting on the instructions of the animals, insects and birds,' the lion began pompously, 'I have been sent to inform you that we are not happy about the behaviour of your second son, Ham. He's upset a good many of us.'

'Oh dear,' said Mr Noah.

'He kicked the rabbit yesterday,' the lion said.

'That's bad,' said Mr Noah.

'And he told the warthog he was surprised God had ever made such an ugly creature,' the lion went on. 'Quite upset his feelings, it did.'

'I'm not surprised,' said Mr Noah.

'I wouldn't let a cub of mine behave as your son does and we think it's high time you did something about it.'

'Yes indeed,' said Mr Noah. 'I'll speak to him at once.'

When Ham came to see him, Mr Noah was firm.

'You've been upsetting the animals and it's got to stop.'

'I haven't done anything,' Ham said.

'I've had the lion here with a list of complaints about your rude behaviour,' said Mr Noah.

'What a cheek! Anyway, who are they to complain? They ought to be grateful to us for saving them!'

'No, Ham,' said Mr Noah. 'Not grateful to *us*. Grateful to God. *He* saved them from the flood. He saved us too and don't you forget it.'

Ham left his father and went to the food store. It was his job that evening to give out the food and drink. But he was far too angry to keep his mind on his work and the animals received only a small amount of food that night and no water at all.

'The service on this voyage really is slipping,' said the emu, poking in her trough.

'Hey, lion, you're the assistant—is there any reason

why our food rations have been cut?' asked the bear bluntly.

'And our water,' called the otter. 'I must have water and my container is quite dry!'

'Here!' said the weasel, angrily pushing the polecat to one side. 'Get your filthy snout out of my feeding trough!'

The polecat pushed him back and in no more than a minute they were fighting round and round the big hall.

'Now then, what's all this?' said Mr Noah, hurrying on to the scene.

'It's him, he started it,' said the weasel.

'No I didn't, he did,' retorted the polecat.

'That's quite enough,' said Mr Noah sternly. 'Lion,

what happened?'

'It's our food,' said the lion. 'Mr Noah, are we running short of food?'

Mr Noah was astonished. 'No, of course not,' he said.

'Or water?' asked the otter anxiously.

'We've plenty of water. God told me exactly how much to take.'

'In that case, why have we all been given small helpings of food and no water this evening?' asked the bear.

'I knew it,' said the monkey in a 'told-you-so' voice. 'I knew it all along. We'll die of starvation and thirst.' He swung himself down from a beam in the roof. 'If we don't all drown first, that is.'

'Nonsense,' said Mr Noah. He looked in their food troughs and water containers. 'How very odd. Leave it with me.'

He went out of the hall and called his three sons.

'Shem, Ham, Japheth, which one of you filled the animals' food troughs and water containers just now?'

'I did, Father,' said Ham.

'Why did you give them short measure and no water?'

'I didn't!' said Ham.

Mr Noah sighed. 'I'm getting tired of all this,' he said. 'Go and give them the right amount of food and water and then come back here to me. And I think you should apologize for letting them go hungry and thirsty,' he added.

Ham was furious. 'Apologize? Me? To *them*? To a load of dirty, smelly animals? You must be joking!'

'I was never more serious,' said Mr Noah.

'Well *you* apologize to them then!' Ham shouted. 'Because I'm not!'

He went out of the cabin, slamming the door behind him. Mr Noah sighed while Shem and Japheth looked at each other.

'We'll do the work, Father,' Shem said.

'If you would help, I'd be grateful,' said Mr Noah. 'But Ham's right in a way. *I* should apologize to the animals, because God put me in charge.'

So Mr Noah went to the big hall and called the animals, insects and birds together.

'I'm very sorry that you have had short rations of food and no water,' he said. 'It won't happen again, I can assure you.'

'Why did it happen at all?' asked the monkey grumpily.

'Because my second son was not thinking about what he was doing,' Mr Noah explained.

'No need to make excuses for him,' called the bear, 'we all know he doesn't like us.'

'If he wasn't *your* son I'd soon make short work of him,' growled the tiger.

Mr Noah was very unhappy when he heard this. He

went to his cabin and talked his problem over with God.

'You see, God, I know it's difficult for him—it is for all of us—cooped up here day after day. And there's nothing more depressing than constant rain, is there? But he really must behave better towards the animals, otherwise we'll have no end of trouble.'

While Mr Noah was talking to God, Ham was talking to his wife.

' . . . and when he said he expected me to *apologize* to the animals . . . Well, that was it. I refuse to do another stroke of work on behalf of that lazy, good-for-nothing bunch of creatures out there.'

'But your father . . .' began his wife.

Ham interrupted. 'Father! You know what I think? I think he's gone off his head. Let's face it, he's six hundred years old. All this worry—building the ark and everything. He's gone round the bend. What those animals need is a strong hand and no nonsense.' He paced up and down the cabin.

'But God . . .' began his wife.

'I know what you're going to say,' Ham said. 'God put my dad in charge, so we've just got to put up with it. Well, you know what I think? I think it was pretty unfair of God to burden the old man with this voyage. A sick old fellow like that . . .'

'He's not sick . . .' protested his wife.

'Whose side are you on?' Ham asked, but did not give

74

her time to reply. 'God should have chosen a younger man, a fitter man—my brother Shem for example... although he's a bit soft like dad. No—God should have chosen *me* to be in charge here.'

There was a knock on the door and Japheth put his head in.

'Father says you're to go and see him in his cabin.'

'Oh, he does, does he...' Ham began.

'Yes,' said Japheth. 'Now.'

A short while later Ham knocked on Mr Noah's cabin door and went inside.

'Now, Father,' he started to say, 'I've been thinking...'

'I've been thinking too,' said his father, cutting him short. 'And, what's more to the point, I've been talking to God. Have *you* talked to God lately?'

'No, but I really don't see...' Ham began.

'That's the problem,' said his father. 'You don't see beyond the end of your nose.'

Ham tried again. 'Look, Dad. I'm sorry if I was rude, but I was upset when you believed a bunch of wild animals rather than me.'

'I believed my own eyes,' said Mr Noah. 'The animals were hungry and thirsty.'

'Yes, but, well... does it matter that much?' Ham said. 'If you ask me, you take far too much trouble over those animals and it's not good for them—or for you for that

75

matter. You're not as young as you were.'

His father was silent.

'Look,' Ham went on. 'God chose us to survive. Our family. So he must think that we're a bit special. He put us in charge of the animals. He gave us power over them.'

'He didn't give us power over all the other creatures on this ark to destroy them,' Mr Noah retorted. 'God wants us to work *with* him to keep all of us alive on this ark and that's a big responsibility. I don't know why God chose us to survive, but I do know that it wasn't because we're cleverer or wiser than anyone else, and we're certainly not cleverer or wiser than God.'

Ham was silent.

Mr Noah looked at him. 'Go away now—and let's have no more talk about my age either. You're as old as you feel and at the moment I don't feel a day older than two hundred and fifty. If God thinks I'm fit to do the job, who am I to argue? He'll give me all the strength I need.'

So Ham went away to his cabin and thought about what his father had said. Then he went to the big hall and told the animals, insects and birds that he was sorry he had been rude to them and sorry that he had not given them enough to eat or drink.

'Quite right too,' growled the bear.

'Let's hope it doesn't happen again,' the emu sniffed.

'But I expect it will,' said the monkey.

'Oh come on now,' said the hedgehog peaceably. 'He said he's sorry, so let's leave it at that.'

So they did leave it at that. Ham no longer grumbled about the animals or shirked his jobs and the animals no longer went short of food or water. And, for a time, there was peace in the ark.

8

THE PIG'S TALE

The ant-eater and the goose both said afterwards that it was all the pigs' own fault for being greedy. The two pigs said that the monkey started it. The monkey said nothing.

The ark had been afloat for a long time as the rain, which God had sent, had flooded the land. God told Mr Noah that the rain would continue for forty days and forty nights. Mr Noah's son, Shem, had made a calendar which hung in the big hall and every morning Mr Noah crossed through the previous day. The chart now had twenty crosses.

'Which means,' said the owl, who liked doing sums, 'that we have had twenty days of rain. In other words,' he paused while he worked out the figures, 'there are twenty days of rain left.'

'You could say,' said the camel slowly, after thinking the matter over, 'that the voyage is half over.'

'Or there's half still to come,' the monkey added gloomily.

'That depends how you look at it.' The eagle spoke from a rafter high up in the big hall. 'To those who look on the bright side of life, we're half-way through this trip. But to those who look on the gloomy side, we've still half of it left.'

'And the second half is bound to be worse,' said the monkey.

'Why's that?' asked the hedgehog.

'Because that's life,' the monkey said.

'I've enjoyed the first half of this trip,' said the dormouse. 'And I expect the second half will be even better.'

'I'm so glad you're happy,' said the monkey sourly. 'Personally I can think of better things to do than being stuck here. Especially with some of our less well-mannered fellow-travellers,' he added, glancing at the two pigs who were busy swilling down their food with many grunts and snuffles of pleasure.

The emu giggled, then sniffed disapprovingly. 'Not very nice,' she said, 'to those of us who were brought up with *manners*.'

'Lowers the tone of the place,' agreed the ant-eater.

The animals all turned to watch the pigs who, having completely cleaned out their own feeding troughs, were now wandering round the other animals' troughs, hungrily eating all the left-overs.

'If you ask *my* opinion,' said one of the geese loudly,

'God shouldn't have allowed greedy animals like them on board.'

'Hush,' said the other goose. 'They'll hear.'

'Serves them right if they do.'

The pigs *had* heard, not just what the goose had said but what everyone else had said as well, and they were very hurt, because pigs are sensitive animals and get upset easily.

'The thing is, they're right,' said the sow that evening to her husband. 'We *are* greedy.'

'No, we're not,' the boar replied. 'I wouldn't call it greedy to have healthy appetites.'

'I'm just so *hungry* all the time,' the sow said unhappily. 'I think we should ask Mr Noah for bigger rations.'

The boar shook his head. 'We can't do that, honey. The other animals wouldn't like it.'

'They don't like us anyway,' said the sow. 'You heard what they said just because we ate their left-overs. And I do hate waste.'

So the pigs continued to eat the animals' left-over food and, before long, some of the animals began to lie in wait for them at mealtimes in order to poke fun.

'Old greedy-guts are on their way,' cawed the jackdaw in a shrill voice.

'They'll burst if they get any fatter,' said the scorpion, staring at the pigs' waddling walk.

The pigs tried to ignore what was being said, but it was hard, especially when the comments became more and more unkind. It was harder still when the animals began to push and jostle them when they were eating.

The crocodile who knocked over their feeding trough said that it was an accident and that he was very sorry—but there was a particularly nasty grin on his face when he said it and he sniggered loudly when he saw the pigs rooting round on the floor for their meal.

That evening the sow was in tears and her husband very angry.

'*Can't* we go to Mr Noah?' sniffed the sow.

'No,' said her husband. 'It would be telling tales, and besides, Mr Noah has enough problems.'

'Well, I can't take much more of this,' the sow wailed.

Not all the animals joined in the teasing.

'Can't you leave them alone?' asked the kangaroo. 'They're only eating what we don't want.'

'It's stealing,' said the goose in a self-righteous voice.

'Aw, come on,' said the kangaroo. 'They're not doing any harm. It's not right to bully them.'

'It's not bullying, it's only teasing,' said the scorpion.

The kangaroo shrugged. 'Same difference,' he said as he hopped away.

'And it's only a bit of fun,' the jackdaw called out.

'Not much fun for the pigs,' muttered the hedgehog, but he was afraid to speak out loud in case the animals turned on him instead.

That evening the cheetah had the idea of hiding the pigs' food. The animals watched in delight as the pigs arrived for their meal, only to stop in dismay when they saw their empty feeding troughs.

'Come on, where have you put it?' demanded the boar.

'Put what?' asked the cheetah, innocently.

'Our food.'

'What food?' asked the ant-eater.

'Why would we want to put your food anywhere?' asked the scorpion.

'Food? Food? I see no food,' called the jackdaw, flapping his wings wildly and laughing so much that he nearly fell off his perch.

'I'm so hungry!' wailed the sow, in tears.

'Serves you right for being so greedy,' said the ant-eater.

It was too all much for the boar. With a squeal of rage he hurled himself at the ant-eater and soon the big hall was filled with fighting animals. Food was thrown everywhere. It plastered the walls and was trodden underfoot as everyone joined in the fight.

'Just *what* is going on here?'

It was Mr Noah.

The fighting stopped and the lion put on his most dignified air. 'There was a small disagreement,' he said loftily. 'And a minor scuffle broke out. It's nothing really.'

'It looks a great deal more than nothing,' said Mr Noah. He looked around at the animals. None of them spoke.

Mr Noah sighed. 'We haven't any food to spare, I'm afraid, so you'd better clean up and if there's anything left worth eating, that will have to do for your supper.'

When he had gone the animals turned on the pigs.

'Thanks to *you* we haven't anything to eat,' said the emu angrily.

The pigs backed away.

'Don't think we'll forget it,' hissed the goose, waving his long neck.

The pigs turned and fled. That night they talked together in whispers.

'What do you think they'll *do*?' asked the sow.

'I don't know, honey.'

'Will they ever let us eat again?'

The boar was silent.

'I'm so hungry my stomach's rumbling,' said the sow.

'Keep quiet a moment,' said the boar. 'I'm thinking.'

'It's so unfair!'

The boar got to his feet. 'Come on,' he said. 'But quietly.'

They set off, tiptoeing along the dark corridors of the ark. The sow followed the boar nervously. Suddenly the boar stopped and the sow bumped into him.

'There!'

'Where?' asked the sow, nursing a sore nose.

'I guessed as much,' said the boar, very pleased with himself.

He nudged open a door and the two pigs walked into the vast store room that held all the food on the ark. The pigs looked around in wonder.

'I guess we'd better eat fast,' said the boar practically. 'We mustn't be caught here.'

So the two pigs ate as fast as they could. They ate and

ate and when they simply could not squeeze in another
mouthful, they staggered back to their sty and fell into a
deep and contented sleep.

The following evening the pigs faced the same
sneering crowd of animals. Once again their food had
been hidden. The sow began to cry.

'Come on, honey,' said the boar. 'We're not stopping
to be treated like this,' and he led her out of the big hall.

That night, when everyone was asleep, they returned
to the store and stuffed themselves full.

When Mr Noah entered the food store the following
day he could not believe his eyes.

'Shem, Ham, Japheth!' he called. 'You haven't been
giving the animals extra food, have you?'

'No, Father.'

'Then why have the food supplies gone down so much?'

'Some of the animals have probably been helping themselves,' said Ham. 'I told you to put a lock on the door.'

'I thought I could trust them,' Mr Noah said sadly.

'Shall I call the animals together, Father?' asked Shem. 'You'll want to find the culprit.'

Mr Noah thought for a moment, then he remembered the fight. He shook his head. 'I think this could be a bit complicated. I'd better talk it over with God.'

That night, when the pigs returned to the store-room, they found Mr Noah waiting for them, a grim expression on his face. The pigs squealed in fright.

'Oh—oh!' said the sow. 'My heart—I'm sure I'm having a heart attack!'

'Just sit down, honey,' said the boar, 'and take it easy.' He turned to Mr Noah. 'I can explain everything,' he said. 'We were just getting our rations.'

'But you are given your rations with the other animals,' Mr Noah said, puzzled.

'Well—not exactly, sir.'

'I think you'd better tell me all about it,' said Mr Noah.

He listened quietly as they spoke and did not interrupt.

'Didn't you realize that you were stealing?' he asked

when they had finished.

The pigs looked at each other. 'I guess we didn't think of it like that,' said the boar.

'Because the animals hid our food, we just thought we were getting what we were entitled to,' said the sow.

Mr Noah looked round the store-room. 'Well, you've eaten your way through a lot more than your fair share. We'll all have to eat a bit less from now on.'

'I'm very sorry,' said the boar. 'It was my idea to come here.'

'I'm sorry too,' said the sow. 'But we were frightened, you see.'

'Why didn't you come and tell me that the animals were bullying you?' Mr Noah asked gently.

There was silence for a moment, then the boar spoke. '*I* said we shouldn't. I was wrong about that too. I'm really sorry.'

The following morning Mr Noah called all the animals, insects and birds together and told them what had happened. He also told them that their food rations would have to be cut for the rest of the journey.

'Those pigs!' muttered the crocodile. 'Just wait 'til I get my teeth into them!'

'You'll leave the pigs alone,' said Mr Noah sternly. 'And it's not all their fault by any means. You're all to blame. The pigs were wrong to steal, but you were cruel to make fun of them and bully and frighten them.'

'Not all of us bullied the pigs,' said the lion with dignity.

'Maybe not,' said Mr Noah. 'But those of you who knew what was going on and did nothing to stop it are almost as bad.'

The animals were silent.

'I've never locked the store-room because I preferred to trust you,' Mr Noah said. 'Do you want me to lock it now?'

'No,' said the hedgehog. 'I'll come and guard it if you like.'

The cheetah laughed. 'Some guard,' he said. He turned to Mr Noah. 'I'm sorry for my part in bullying the pigs. You're right. We're all to blame. I'll make sure it doesn't happen again and I'm sure you don't need to lock the store-room.'

The rest of the animals agreed, and at feeding time there was peace in the ark.

'But I'm still hungry,' wailed the sow.

'Here,' said the hedgehog, going up to her. 'You can have some of my food. I don't need as much as you.'

'Thank you,' said the sow quietly.

And she dried her eyes and was content.

9

THE SPIDER'S TALE

When all the animals, insects and birds were queueing to
enter the ark, Mr Noah looked at them and was amazed at
the variety of creatures that existed in the world.

First there were the animals. Big ones and small ones,
wild ones and tame, nice ones and nasty ones, tall and
short, ugly and beautiful, clever and stupid. The animals
walked, jumped, hopped, ran and slithered up the ramp
and into the ark.

Then there were the birds. Chirping and cheeping,
squawking and squeaking, fluttering and cooing. Large
birds and small. Fierce and gentle. The air was alive with
the beat of their wings and the chatter of their voices as
they flew into the ark.

And lastly came the insects. Creeping and crawling,
wriggling and squirming, flying and jumping, the insects
came in all shapes and sizes and the look of some of them
sent shivers down Mr Noah's back.

But of all the creatures that came into the ark, none

upset Mr Noah as much as the two black, hairy, long-legged spiders.

'You see, God,' Mr Noah said, once he was safe in his cabin. 'I'm scared of spiders.'

But God already knew.

Once the door of the ark was closed and Mr Noah was busy with his daily jobs, he tried not to think too much about the spiders.

'After all,' said his wife, 'they're God's creatures just like you and me and perhaps they're scared of us.'

Which was all very true, but it did not help Mr Noah.

To make matters worse, the spiders liked exploring. They explored all over the ark, and especially—or so it seemed to Mr Noah—inside his cabin.

'Please,' Mr Noah said after he had found them scuttling across the floor. 'Would you mind not coming in here without knocking?'

'Why?' asked one of the spiders.

'Because it's private. All the other animals knock if they want to see me.'

'But we don't want to see you particularly,' said the other spider. 'We just like exploring.'

'Besides,' said the first spider. 'We can't knock. Our legs wouldn't be strong enough for you to hear.'

Mr Noah looked at the large number of black legs around the body of the spider and tried not to shudder.

'You don't like us, do you?' said the second spider suddenly.

'Whatever makes you say that?' Mr Noah asked. 'Of course I like you.'

'No, you don't,' the spider persisted. 'Don't think we haven't noticed.'

'If God hadn't told you to look after us, you'd probably squash us,' added the first spider. 'Lots of humans do.'

'No, I wouldn't,' said Mr Noah, but he did not sound convincing.

'It's all right,' the first spider said kindly. 'We understand.'

'I don't know why people don't like us,' the second spider said thoughtfully. 'We're really useful and there are lots of uglier animals and insects than us.'

'I'm sorry,' said Mr Noah. 'I don't know why it is, but I can't help it.'

'We can't help what we look like,' said the first spider. 'I might not have wanted to be born with all these hairy legs.' She waved them around. 'I might have wanted to be like you...' she looked at him for a moment, '... or perhaps something rather nicer-looking.'

'And let's face it, we don't harm anyone,' said the second. 'Apart from insects, of course.'

'Come on,' said his wife. 'It's no use staying here. I know when we're not wanted.'

So the two spiders scuttled away and Mr Noah watched them go, glad that they were leaving his cabin, but feeling rather guilty all the same.

'Why am I frightened of them, God?' Mr Noah asked. 'I mean, they're quite right, there are lots of uglier creatures on board but they don't make me shudder and want to run away.'

Just then there was an almighty crash and the whole ark shook.

'Speak to you later, God,' said Mr Noah, and he rushed out of his cabin. The corridor was full of animals and everyone was talking at once.

'He's dead, he's dead, I know he is!' shrieked the emu.

'I just can't stand the sight of blood!' quavered the peacock.

'Stand back,' called the tiger, 'give him some room!'

'I always did say those stairs were a death trap,' said the monkey to anyone who would listen. 'Knew it soon as I came on board.'

Mr Noah knelt over the body of the horse.

'He's not dead, is he?' asked the mare, his wife.

'No,' said Mr Noah, after a quick examination. 'He's not dead. But he's knocked himself out and cut one of his legs rather badly. Shem, go and fetch some water, will you, and tell your mother. She's good at nursing. We'll clean him up and then carry him to his stable.' He turned to the animals. 'How did it happen?'

'I don't know,' said the tiger.

'He slipped,' said the bear. 'Silly thing to do, but it could have happened to anyone.'

'It's those stairs,' said the goose. 'I agree with the monkey. I've always thought they were dangerous. I'm just surprised it hasn't happened before.'

The horse did not come round until late in the evening. When he did, he had a bad headache, which was not surprising. Over the next few days a constant stream of animals, insects and birds came to visit the patient and cheer him up.

Some of the birds sang to soothe his sore head; the squirrel brought him nuts from his private store; the giraffe told long and not very funny stories (which brought back the horse's headache), and the koala bear and the guinea-pig, finding his straw warm and comfortable, moved into his stable. The horse began to feel better, but the cuts on his leg would not heal.

Mrs Noah tried all the ointments she had brought with her but nothing seemed to work. After a while the cuts became infected and the horse grew very ill.

'Good fresh air and sunshine is what he needs,' Mrs Noah said, shaking her head. 'There's nothing more I can do.'

Mr Noah went to see the sick horse who lay sweating

in his stable. His eyes were glazed and his coat was matted and rough to the touch.

'I'm not going to die, am I?' asked the horse in a weak voice.

'No, of course not,' Mr Noah said reassuringly. 'I shall go and talk to God.'

But Mr Noah was very worried.

'What shall I do, God?' he asked. 'How can I save the horse? If he dies there'll be no more horses in the world once the rain stops and the flood goes down. You can't mean that to happen, God. Can't you work a miracle?'

Suddenly Mr Noah felt something tickling the back of his hand. He looked down and jumped in fright. One of the spiders was walking across his hand and up his arm! He shook his arm vigorously and the spider gracefully spun itself to the floor.

'I told you not to come in here without knocking,' Mr Noah said, angry because he had been frightened.

'We did knock, but you didn't hear us,' said the spider.

'So we had to come in, because it's all rather urgent,' explained his wife.

'What do you mean?' asked Mr Noah.

'The horse, of course,' she said patiently. 'You want to save the horse, don't you?'

'I was just talking to God about it when you interrupted me,' Mr Noah replied.

'Exactly,' said the first spider. 'So let's go.'

'Go?' asked Mr Noah. 'Where?'

'To see the horse. Come on, we're wasting time.'

Mr Noah looked at the spiders' black, hairy bodies. 'But what can you do?' he asked in astonishment.

'Nothing if we don't hurry,' said the first spider, already at the door.

The horse was tossing and turning, making small sounds. His wife lay beside him and licked him gently from time to time. Mrs Noah kept the straw piled high around him and many of the animals, insects and birds in the ark were assembled outside, silently watching.

The spiders scuttled through the crowd and crawled onto the horse's leg. The horse twitched a little.

'Now then, dear, it's all right,' said the first spider in a comfortable voice. 'We're not going to hurt you. We're just going to weave a web of the finest silk threads to cover your bad leg and that will make it comfortable.' She turned to her husband. 'You start that end and I'll start this.'

'Hmmph,' said the monkey. '*That* won't do any good!'

'Have you got a better idea?' asked the dormouse.

'Well...'

'Keep quiet then,' growled the tiger.

The monkey and all the animals kept quiet as the two spiders spun their silken web over and around the cuts on the horse's leg. They made a gentle buzzing sound and the horse lay still. Soon the horse's leg was covered in a

shimmering web of silver strands. The spiders made silken ladders for themselves, climbed down, and settled on the straw beside the horse.

'What happens next?' asked the tiger in a loud whisper.

'Nothing,' said the spider. 'This isn't a circus. The horse needs peace and quiet. I suggest you all go away.'

Some of the animals did go, but most of them stayed, falling asleep one by one. The horse fell asleep too. His breathing was noisy and harsh-sounding. By the middle

of the night the only ones awake were the guinea-pig, who only ever slept for a minute or two at a time, the two spiders, and Mr and Mrs Noah, who spent the night talking to God.

Just before dawn the horse's breathing changed to a deep, peaceful sound and his coat began to regain its rich brown colour. Mrs Noah touched it gently.

'His skin feels warm and smooth,' she said quietly. 'The fever's gone and he's getting better.'

Mr Noah looked at the two spiders and, for once, he

did not shudder when he saw their black, hairy bodies and he was not frightened by their long furry legs.

He held out his hands and the spiders crawled onto them.

'Thank you,' said Mr Noah. 'I'll never be frightened of you again.'

10
THE MONKEY'S TALE

The ark, which Mr Noah had built to God's instructions, had been afloat for over twenty days. The small ship was wrapped in swirling grey mist as it drifted around an endless sea. The rain continued to fall, day after day after day.

Inside the ark, the animals, insects and birds began to wonder whether the rain would ever stop and whether the flood would go down so that they could live on dry land again.

'I'd just like to see a bit of sun and blue sky,' sighed the lark. 'This rain gets me down.'

'Give us a song to cheer us up,' said the camel, but the lark shook her head and went to perch high in the rafters where she could stare out of the window at the slanting rain.

Some of the animals hibernated, tucking themselves into corners and sleeping through the long days and nights. Everyone found life on board the ark more and more difficult.

'We'll be stuck on this ark for ever,' the monkey said gloomily. 'You mark my words.'

'Do you really think so?' the goat asked anxiously.

The camel sniffed. 'Don't take any notice of him. He always looks on the black side of things.'

'*Is* there another side?' the monkey asked sarcastically.

'If we're stuck on this ark, what about food?' asked the pig. 'What happens when we come to the end of the food?'

'We starve,' said the monkey.

'Oh dear,' said the pig, turning pale.

The monkey hunched himself into his corner. 'This whole trip was doomed from the start,' he said. 'It was just a crazy idea of Mr Noah's.'

'But it wasn't Mr Noah's idea, it was God's idea,' said the dog. 'And anyway, it's only going to rain for forty days. That what Mr Noah says and he got that straight from God.'

The monkey gave a secret little smile. 'Suppose Mr Noah got it wrong?'

'He couldn't have,' said the dog.

'He might have,' the monkey persisted. 'He's only a human after all, and they're not anything like as clever as they make out.'

'They're a great deal cleverer than you,' said the dog, bristling.

'Oh, we all know how well *you* get on with them,' sneered the monkey.

'Mr Noah is a good man,' said the dormouse who was lying half-asleep on some straw.

'I never said he wasn't. But, good or not, he could still have got it wrong.' The monkey looked round the circle of doubtful faces. 'That's why I'm saying we'll be on this ark for ever.'

There was a dismayed silence.

Then the bear said bluntly, 'You like upsetting things and making mischief, don't you?'

'Me?' said the monkey, raising his eyebrows. 'We have to look at the facts, don't we?' And he looked round at the crowd of gloomy faces.

The giant tortoise, who seldom spoke, slowly lifted his great head and looked at the monkey.

'I have lived longer than you, monkey,' he said in his deep voice. 'In fact, I have lived longer than you all. I can remember times when the rain came and the rivers rose and flooded the land. They were terrible times. But in the end the rain stopped and the waters went down. And I can remember times of drought, dreadful times when everything was dry and all living creatures cried out for water. But the rain came in the end. And this flood will pass also. Everything passes in time.'

'But this time it might be different,' said the monkey.

The giant tortoise stared at the monkey. His wise old

eyes in his lined and wrinkled face were stern. 'I think not,' he said.

'Well, all we can do is trust in Mr Noah and hope that we survive,' said the dog.

The monkey turned on him. 'I've no hope at all that we'll survive, and I don't trust Mr Noah or anyone else,' he said. 'Anyway, I'm tired of all this talking. You believe what you want. I don't believe in what I can't see and I can't see any sign of the rain stopping.'

The days passed and the rain showed no sign of stopping. The atmosphere in the ark grew more and more gloomy. Everyone was affected. Arguments and fights broke out among the animals, the birds refused to sing and Mr Noah's sons and their wives rushed through their jobs and spent as much time as they could shut up in their cabins. Meanwhile the monkey went around with an 'I told you so' expression on his face. This made even the gentlest animals want to bite him.

Even Mr Noah became gloomy and began to have doubts. He wondered whether he *had* got it wrong after all. Maybe he had not understood God. Perhaps the rain would not stop after forty days and then where would they be? A small, frail ark sailing for ever without food, without water and with a cargo of increasingly hungry animals. Mr Noah shuddered at the thought.

Perhaps, Mr Noah thought at last, *God* might have got it wrong. He tried talking to God, but God must have been busy because he did not answer.

Mr Noah stopped trying to cheer up the animals, he felt so miserable himself. He spent more and more time in his cabin thinking about the life he used to have before the flood. He remembered the house he had lived in with his wife and sons and thought longingly of his fine vineyards. His wine had been the best in the neighbourhood. Mr Noah wondered whether he would ever make wine again and whether life would ever be the same again.

There was a knock on his door. It was the lion.

'I'm sorry to trouble you, Mr Noah, but you must

come quickly.'

'Why? What's happened?'

'It's the frogs.'

Mr Noah left his cabin and hurried down the corridor, the lion at his heels.

'They've hopped on to the roof and they're threatening to jump off.'

'Why?'

'Because the monkey says it'll never stop raining and we're stuck on this ark for ever and the frogs said that if that's the case they'd rather die now and get it over with.'

'Oh dear.'

'Yes, and the monkey says perhaps we should all do that. But *he* doesn't seem too anxious to jump off himself. Personally I think it's all a trick to get more space and more food for himself—I wouldn't trust that monkey an inch. But anyway, some of the animals are already

climbing onto the roof.'

When Mr Noah and the lion reached the top of the ark they found not only the frogs, but also the ostrich perched on the roof while a host of animals, insects and birds crowded the corridor. Mr Noah put his head through the trapdoor and peered out.

'Whatever are you doing?' he asked.

'We think the monkey's right,' croaked the frog. 'It'll never stop raining and there's no point going on and on hoping that everything will come right. So we've decided to end it now.'

'Please come down,' Mr Noah pleaded. 'Why listen to what the monkey says?'

'Because it makes sense,' said the other frog.

'But God makes sense too,' said Mr Noah. 'And we have his promise that the rain will stop.'

'How do we know that?' sneered the monkey, who was down in the corridor. 'We only have *your* word for it. And we haven't seen much of you lately, have we? Perhaps you've been doubting God as well?'

Mr Noah turned red, for that was exactly what he had been doing. But he answered stoutly.

'Look, I know it's difficult. But we have to trust God. That's the only hope we have.'

Suddenly the ostrich shrieked. 'Help! I don't like heights!'

'Then why did you climb up there in the first place,

you silly creature?' asked the lion crossly.

'Save me, Mr Noah!' screeched the ostrich. 'I don't want to die!'

The frog gulped. 'Neither do I,' he said suddenly.

Mr Noah held out his arms and caught the ostrich, who wriggled and squirmed. Eventually he managed to get the bird back into the ark. Slowly the frogs followed and the trapdoor was shut. The animals returned to the big hall and Mr Noah went to his cabin.

'God, are you there?' he asked.

'I'm always here,' God said.

'They're saying that this rain is never going to end,' said Mr Noah unhappily.

'I know what they are saying,' said God.

'What can I do about it?'

'Trust me,' God replied.

'I do.'

'Do you? What about your doubts? What about your vineyard, Noah, and your worries about the future?'

Mr Noah was silent.

'The animals will never believe you unless you yourself believe what I say.'

Mr Noah looked down.

'Noah,' said God. 'It all depends on you. I can't make you trust me.'

There was a long silence. At last Mr Noah spoke in a small voice.

'If I hadn't trusted you, Lord, I wouldn't be here now. I'd have drowned long ago.' He looked up. 'I'm sorry for doubting you.'

'There's nothing wrong in having doubts, Noah, so don't apologize,' said God.

Mr Noah went to the big hall and called everyone together. He cleared his throat and held up his hand for silence.

'God has promised that we'll be saved, and God does not break his promises,' he said firmly. 'Just be patient a little longer and don't lose hope.'

'All very fine words,' the monkey sneered. 'But it hasn't stopped the rain.'

The eagle suddenly swept down into the hall.

'The rain *has* stopped,' he called out.

He flew up to the trapdoor and pushed it wide open. And for the first time for forty days and forty nights, the animals, insects and birds felt cold fresh *dry* air stream down on their upturned faces.

'Look!' cried the skylark, her face uplifted to catch the breeze. 'There's blue sky!'

The clouds that had wrapped the earth in a grey mist were blowing away, driven by winds that sent them scudding across the sky. One patch of blue appeared, then another and soon the whole sky was radiant with colour, blue and red and gold, as the setting sun sank towards the horizon.

One after another the birds flew up and out of the ark, singing for joy. The light of the sun shone on their faces, and their wings seemed tipped with gold.

Some animals and insects clambered on to the roof, holding on to each other tightly to make sure they did not fall off. The ones left inside began to dance and sing and Mr and Mrs Noah and their family thanked God for ending the rain.

And the monkey?

The monkey went quietly to his sleeping place and no one missed him at all.

11

THE ELEPHANT'S TALE

The morning after the rain had stopped, the lion woke Mr Noah early.

'Excuse me, Mr Noah, but we've had a check and everyone's present and correct.'

Mr Noah blinked. 'Pleasant and...?'

'*Present*, Mr Noah. Ready and waiting.'

Mr Noah shook his head and tried to wake up.

'Waiting for what?'

'The door to open, of course.'

'What door?'

'The door to the ark. Will you open it yourself or will we have the pleasure of seeing God perform the grand opening ceremony?'

Mr Noah got out of bed and groped for his sandals. 'I think I'd better come,' he said.

The corridor outside his cabin was full of hurrying animals, crawling insects and flying birds. The babble of noise grew louder as Mr Noah approached the big hall.

Inside, he found a crowd of excited animals, insects and birds all milling around in front of the big closed door of the ark. Even his sons and their wives were waiting eagerly, clutching their few belongings in their hands.

A cheer went up as he appeared. Someone started to sing 'For he's a jolly good fellow' at the back of the hall.

'C'mon, Mr Noah, stir yourself!' called the fox.

'Open the door, Mr Noah!' cried the jackal. 'I want to go hunting again!'

Mr Noah blinked at all the excitement.

'I'm sorry,' he said, 'but there's been some mistake.'

'Mistake?'

The singing stopped and the shouts died away.

'What sort of a mistake?' asked the leopard slowly.

'Didn't you tell us that God said it would rain for forty days and forty nights?' asked the jackal.

'Well, yes,' agreed Mr Noah.

'And during that time the earth would be flooded, but all of us here in this ark would be saved from the flood?'

'Of course.'

'And after forty days and forty nights the rain would stop?'

'Absolutely.'

The jackal thrust his face close to Mr Noah's.

'Well, the rain's stopped now, hasn't it? So what's to stop us from leaving, eh?'

Mr Noah took a step back. 'Just take a look outside.'

The eagle, who had been keeping to his perch high up in the rafters of the hall and close to the trapdoor, looked down on the assembled group.

'We can't leave,' he said. 'If we opened the door now, the ark would fill with water and sink. We're still floating on an endless sea and there is no land at all in sight.'

Everyone heard this in silence. The panther, who had been pacing up and down impatiently, turned to Mr Noah.

'Well?' he asked in a silky voice.

'Well what? What the eagle said is right. We can't leave the ark yet.'

'How long?' snapped the fox.

Mr Noah shook his head. 'I don't know.'

'Didn't God tell you how long it would be before we could leave?' asked the panther.

'No. I'm afraid he didn't.'

'Then I suggest you go and ask him,' said the jackal.

Mr Noah was worried as he spoke to God. 'Don't get me wrong, God. I'm not asking for myself, but there are some very angry animals out there and I'm not sure how I'll manage to keep them quiet unless you can give me a hint about how long it will be before the flood-waters subside.'

But God shook his head. 'I'm sorry, Noah, I can't tell you that. I can't tell you everything. You will just have to be patient and wait.'

'Wait?,' squeaked Mr Noah in a frightened voice. 'Wait? Well, that's all very well, God, and I'm happy enough to wait, as you know, but what do I tell the animals? I can't ask *them* to be patient. You don't know them like I do.'

God smiled. 'The animals will surprise you,' he said.

'That's what I'm afraid of,' Mr Noah said darkly, but God spoke no more.

When Mr Noah told the animals, insects and birds what God had said, there were angry faces and even

angrier voices.

'False pretences, that's what it is. You got us here under false pretences,' said the ant-eater.

'Forty days is what you said and forty days is what I understood,' the jackal complained.

'I think, Mr Noah, you have some explaining to do,' said the panther in a dangerously quiet voice and the animals murmured agreement. They began to close in on Mr Noah in a menacing way, but instead of being frightened, Mr Noah grew angry.

'Just a minute!' he said loudly. 'Just a minute! All I ever said was that God wanted to save two of each of you from the flood. He told me to build this ark and said that once the door was shut, it would rain for forty days and forty nights until the earth and all its wickedness was wiped out. God never gave a time limit as to how long we'd have to stay on the ark. If God *does* know he's not saying, and why should he? It's not my fault that you can't leave the ark.'

The animals were quiet now. Mr Noah went on. 'Look, I know it's a disappointment, but be sensible. Now that the rain's stopped, the flood-waters will go down eventually.'

'It's like a prison sentence without knowing when you'll be let out,' muttered the rat in a dejected voice.

The emu sniffed. 'Never having been in prison, I really couldn't say,' she said. She turned to Mr Noah. 'I still think it's your fault. It really is too bad of you.'

Mr Noah sighed. 'Just be thankful that you're alive and safe.'

There was some restless murmuring in the hall, then the elephant spoke. 'That's very true, Mr Noah. We *should* be grateful. And my wife and I thank you for saving us from the flood.'

The elephant's wife looked round the hall. 'I think, instead of sitting here complaining, we ought to do something with the time we still have together on the ark.'

'Like what?' asked the fox abruptly.

'Like ... um ... like ... having a party,' she said. 'And, if you all agree, we will organize it.'

The tiger brightened up. 'I'll help,' he said.

'And me,' said the giraffe.

'Count us in,' called the birds.

The tiger smiled happily. 'We'll form a committee.'

'Thank you, God,' said Mr Noah quietly. 'You said the animals would surprise me.'

Plans for the party were soon under way. Suggestions for entertainment poured in. The committee took lots of decisions and the elephants—who did most of the work—could be seen, and heard, thundering from one end of the ark to the other. The party was going to last for a whole day. It would include games and competitions, side-shows and displays.

'If you like,' said the peacock graciously, 'I'll display my beautiful tail once an hour for those who wish to admire it.'

'Thank you very much,' said the elephant.

The mandrill laughed. 'In that case I'll display my beautiful red and pink bottom,' he said rudely. 'I bet I get as many admirers as the peacock.'

It took both elephants and the entire committee a long time to soothe the peacock's ruffled feelings.

The next day, every corner of the ark was filled with animals, insects and birds practising for the party. The elephants went round with their long trunks in the air and worried expressions on their faces.

'Food,' said the elephant. 'I know food is rationed, but we do need something a bit special for the party.'

He went off in search of Mr Noah.

'Notices,' said the elephant's wife. 'We need notices about the party.'

'Why?' asked the tiger. 'Everyone knows about it.'

'Just in case they don't,' she said. 'Who can write?'

'Who can read?' asked the monkey, who had been keeping out of all the preparations.

'Mr Noah's sons can write,' said the tiger. 'I'll go and ask them.'

Then the elephant's wife had another thought. 'We must clean and decorate the big hall,' she said. 'Now let me think...'

The night before the party when most of the animals, insects and birds were safely asleep, the committee met in the big hall. They worked hard and by morning the place was transformed. The floor shone with wax provided by the bees and polished by the elephants and tigers. The walls had been hung with lacy webs made by the spiders. The eating place groaned with extra rations of food and everything shimmered in the glow worm's soft light.

As the animals, insects and birds entered the hall on the following day, they gasped in amazement.

Then Mr Noah and his family arrived.

'This is wonderful,' said Mr Noah, his face beaming with pleasure. 'Why didn't you tell us what you'd planned? We would have come and helped.'

'We wanted it to be a surprise for you and Mrs Noah as much as for everyone else,' said the elephant. 'It's our way of saying thank you for all you have done for us.'

Before long, everyone had settled down to the serious business of eating. Once the feast was over the competitions began. The polar bear challenged the tiger for the title 'Strongest Animal on the Ark'. They lifted the two hippopotami who were very heavy. The cheetah challenged any animal to a race round the hall for the title 'Fastest Animal on the Ark'. Not to be outdone, the sloth, the tortoise and the snail entered a competition for the title 'Slowest Animal on the Ark' and were still finishing the course two days after the party had ended!

The termites demonstrated their house-building skills, the woodpeckers pecked wood, the kangaroo beat his own record for the long jump, while the peacock graciously showed off his tail. The mandrill did not show off anything and the lion, with great dignity, acted as Master of Ceremonies.

Then came the entertainment. The chameleon, in a very dramatic performance, changed colour from green to red to brown. This was followed by the snake who shed his entire skin. The giraffe told long and not very funny stories and the penguins, neat and tidy in black and white, did a song and dance routine.

The donkey did a juggling act and was applauded every time he dropped a plate—which was very often—and everyone gasped at the magpie's amazing conjuring tricks as he made various objects disappear. The spiders performed a trapeze act on fine webs they had woven for the purpose and a mixed choir of birds, conducted by the blackbird, sang a medley of songs for the audience to join in.

At the end they all clapped loudly, for a long, long time. Even the crocodile—who was not the easiest of animals to please—said that he hadn't enjoyed himself so much for years.

After the entertainment came the dancing. The wolf asked the sheep to dance, the leopard could be seen with the cow, and the fox bent his head politely to listen to something the rabbit was saying as they danced together. The flamingo gave a solo performance and the only moment of panic came when the two elephants, flushed with success, danced too heavily at the far end of the hall, causing the ark to dip and wobble in the water. The animals dragged them back to the centre and the dancing continued until late into the night.

There was a magic about that party and no one wanted it to end. Afloat on a black sea, the small ark was filled with laughter and song and a feeling of goodwill among the humans, animals, insects and birds that had never been there before.

'It's been a lovely evening,' said the elephant's wife, and there were tears in her eyes.

'Yes it has,' said the dormouse. He sighed. 'If only it could always be like this.'

'Yes,' agreed Mr Noah. 'If only it could.'

12

THE DOVE'S TALE

'I do feel ill,' said the kangaroo, as the ark dipped and bobbed on the water.

'You shouldn't have jumped about so much last night,' said the hippopotamus. 'Made me quite dizzy watching you.'

It was the day after the party in which the animals, insects and birds on board the ark had celebrated the stopping of the rain.

'*I* didn't jump about and I feel ill too,' groaned the giraffe. 'What's happened to the floor? It's going up and down.'

'It's the after-effects of the party,' said the lion, who was slumped against the wall, looking quite pale and unlike himself. 'Why is it that one always feels unwell after a party?' He stopped suddenly. 'Oh dear,' he said in a quavering voice. 'I do feel sick.'

The eagle flew in through the trapdoor in the roof of the ark. 'It's wonderful out there,' he said. 'There's a fine, strong wind blowing. And there are some huge waves. The sea's very rough.'

But few of the animals heard him. They were feeling far too ill.

The wind blew for several days, tossing the little ark up and down on stormy waters. Almost all the animals were seasick, many of the insects felt off-colour and Mr Noah, Mrs Noah and their entire family kept to their cabins as much as they could.

'But just think,' said Mr Noah, trying to keep cheerful as he tottered around with a green face, 'this wind will soon dry up the flood.'

'Can't be soon enough for me,' groaned the dog, who did not like travelling on boats at the best of times.

But although the wind was strong, no land appeared, and the sea of flood-water on which the ark floated seemed as deep as ever.

Then the wind dropped. The scudding clouds cleared away and a hot sun shone out of a blue sky. Each day the birds streamed out of the ark and circled high in the air, searching for land. The animals began to feel better and those who could swim dived off the side of the ark and searched underwater. Those who could neither fly nor swim took it in turns to sit up on the roof and enjoy the fresh air.

'I do like lying in the sun,' said the tiger, stretching out on the roof of the ark.

'Be careful!' squeaked the hedgehog. 'You nearly knocked me off.'

'Sorry,' said the tiger. 'I wonder why Mr Noah didn't make the roof of the ark any bigger? There would have been room for more of us up here.'

The eagle, who was circling above them, laughed. 'I don't suppose Mr Noah was thinking about sunbathing when he built the ark,' he said.

'It's all right for you,' the tiger grumbled. 'You can fly.'

The giraffe poked his long neck through the trapdoor.

'Come on,' he said to the tiger. 'Shift yourself. You've been up here twice as long as anyone else. Get down and let someone else have a chance.'

The tiger stood and stretched. 'Oh, very w...e...ll!'

His voice ended in a shriek as the ark shuddered and jerked. The tiger lost his footing and slid to the very edge of the roof.

'Help ...!'

The hedgehog, the giraffe and the monkey grabbed at his tail while the birds circled low, uttering cries of distress.

Mr Noah jumped on to the roof and helped pull the tiger to safety.

'What happened?' the tiger asked, badly shaken.

'We must have hit something,' Mr Noah said.

'An iceberg,' called the polar bear, who was in the water enjoying a swim. 'Have we hit an iceberg, Mr Noah?'

'No, of course not,' said Mr Noah. 'It's far too warm for icebergs. I think it must be land of some sort. Perhaps the top of a mountain.'

'Is the ark all right?' asked the dormouse, anxiously poking his head through the trapdoor. 'It hasn't been damaged, has it?'

'I'll go and look,' said the polar bear. He dived out of sight but surfaced a moment later on the other side of the ark. 'No damage, but we're stuck on something,' he called.

'Isn't it exciting?' said the monkey sarcastically. 'I can't wait for the ark to capsize.'

'Oh shut up,' said the tiger irritably, and went down

to the big hall to recover.

That evening the birds met on the roof.

'It's wonderful to be flying again,' said the nightingale. 'I feel as if the whole world has just been born.'

'I didn't want to come back,' said the seagull. 'I wanted to fly on and on across the sea.'

'Well, why did you come back?' asked the raven. He looked round at the birds. 'Why did any of us come back? We've got wings, haven't we? We're not tied to this ark. There must be land somewhere and we can fly away to find it.'

'I don't think that's right,' said the dove in her soft voice. 'We can't just fly off and leave everyone behind. That would be selfish.'

'Why should we worry about everyone else?' asked the raven. 'When have they worried about us?'

'That's not the point,' said the dove gently. 'We're all in this together.'

'No, we're not,' said the raven. 'We're all in this because Mr Noah was told by God to save two of each of us from the flood. It was just chance that we were chosen.'

'Mr Noah has fed us and looked after us,' said the eagle.

'And kept us safe from being eaten,' said the sparrow.

'All right,' said the raven. 'Mr Noah has been good to us. But I don't see that staying here when we don't need to is going to help Mr Noah. Look at it this way. Aren't

we the ones who are selfish by staying and using the food and space that others need?'

The birds murmured as they thought about this. Then the eagle spoke harshly. 'You're just trying to find excuses for going off and doing what you want to do!'

'No, I'm not!' said the raven angrily.

Mr Noah put his head through the trapdoor.

'There you all are, I was looking for you. I need your help. I'd like one of you to fly away from the ark to see if there is any sight of land. Would anyone volunteer?

'As the bird with the keenest eyesight...' the eagle began.

'I'll go,' said the raven quickly.

The blackbird looked at him. 'You won't come back,' he said. 'You just told us so.'

'I will,' said the raven. He turned to Mr Noah. 'Honestly, Mr Noah, I will come back.'

Mr Noah looked round the circle of birds. No one

spoke.

He turned to the raven. 'Very well,' he said. 'I trust you.'

The following day the raven flew out of the ark, high into the blue sky. The ark grew smaller and smaller until it was just a tiny speck on the wide sea.

'I'm free!' called the raven, but no one heard him.

He flew higher still and the ark disappeared from sight.

'Oh, how good to get away!' the raven thought. 'How good to be flying in the silent air with the sun on my wings...'

He flew on and on.

'Just a little further...' he thought. 'There'll be land a little further. If I do find land, should I go back to the ark and tell them, or keep it to myself?' he wondered. 'I could be the first bird in the world. I could be the *only* bird in the world...'

The daylight faded and the raven grew tired and hungry.

'Perhaps I'll go back tonight and have a rest and some food and then try again tomorrow,' he thought.

He turned round, but the sky had grown very dark and the sea even darker. Where was the ark? The raven was afraid.

'I shouldn't have been so keen to go,' he said out loud, but no one heard him.

'I've been very selfish,' he said, but the wind carried his words away.

'I wish I could find my way home,' he called in despair.

Inside the ark, Mr Noah was growing more and more worried.

'I shouldn't have sent him, Lord,' he said. 'The other birds told me he wouldn't come back. I shouldn't have trusted him.'

'It would be a sad world without trust,' said God. 'You did what you thought right, Noah. Now go to bed and get some rest and leave the raven to my care.'

But although Mr Noah went to bed, he could not sleep, and the following morning he was up at dawn, standing on the roof of the ark, looking anxiously into the sky.

Suddenly he shouted out loud. There, in the distance, flying very, very slowly, was the raven. He landed with a thud on the roof of the ark.

'I'm sorry,' he gasped. 'I wasn't going to come back at all ... then I was hungry ... and tired ... lost my way ...'

'Did you see any land?' asked the eagle, who was circling above.

The raven slowly shook his head. 'No land ...'

'Never mind,' said Mr Noah. 'I'm just glad you did come back.'

He gave the raven food and put him to bed. It was some days before Mr Noah asked for another volunteer to fly off in search of land.

'Do you still trust us?' asked the eagle slowly. 'We feel that the raven let us all down.'

'I trust you,' said Mr Noah.

The birds were silent for a moment, then the dove stirred.

'If you and God think it right for one of us to go, then I volunteer,' she said in her gentle voice.

'Thank you,' said Mr Noah.

For a while longer they waited and watched, but the flood-waters seemed as high as ever and no land appeared, so at last the dove flew out of the ark. She circled once, twice, three times and her eyes were dazzled by the sun. She flew in great sweeping arcs, backwards and forwards across the sea but there was no sign of land. At last it began to grow dark and the dove returned to the ark. She was so tired that Mr Noah had to hold her in his hands and help her inside.

'There is no land as far as I can see,' she said wearily, 'and I travelled for miles.'

'We'll wait a bit longer,' said Mr Noah. 'As long as the sun shines the flood-waters will dry up.'

The sun carried on shining and the animals carried on taking turns to bask in the warm air on the roof of the ark. The insects did what insects usually do and the birds flew around, strengthening their wings for the return to the world.

Seven days later the dove set out again from the ark. She was stronger now and could fly further. She flew low, skimming the surface of the water as she watched for any sign of land. All day she flew but she could see nothing.

'Oh dear,' she thought. 'I did so want to take good news back to Mr Noah.'

The sun slipped lower and lower in the sky until it disappeared below the horizon. Disappointed, the dove turned to go. She flew slowly, still searching in the red afterglow of sunset.

Then she spotted it. There was something sticking up out of the water. She flew down to look. It was a branch, a branch of a tree and on it were some leaves. The dove plucked one and flew back in triumph to the ark.

There was enormous excitement at her return.

'What is it?' asked the polar bear, prodding it with a curious paw.

'It's a leaf, you fool,' said the goat.

'I can see it's a leaf, but what sort?' asked the polar

bear. 'I've never seen anything quite like it before.'

'It's from an olive tree,' said the donkey. 'There's a lot of them where I come from.'

'What does it mean?' asked the emu excitedly.

'It means land,' said Mr Noah. 'It means that the water on earth has gone down and the tree-tops are above the water.'

'So can we get off the ark?' asked the hedgehog.

'Soon, soon,' said Mr Noah.

He waited another seven days before doing anything more.

'Better be safe than sorry,' he said.

This time he sent both doves. 'I think you should both go,' he said. 'Because if you do find land, there's no point in your returning here.'

The two doves went round the ark saying goodbye to the other birds as well as the animals and insects.

'You know, I feel quite upset at the thought of leaving,' said one of the doves. 'In some ways I almost hope we don't find land, although I know that's silly.'

Last of all the doves went to Mr Noah.

'If we don't come back, Mr Noah, we'll never forget you,' they said.

'And I'll never forget you,' said Mr Noah. He took them gently in both his hands. 'I'll always think of you as messengers of peace, for you brought the news that God has kept his promise.'

The doves flew up through the trapdoor. They circled low over the ark, calling their goodbyes, then they soared up into the air and were gone.

They never came back.

A few days later Mr Noah looked out of the trapdoor in the roof of the ark and saw dry land all about him!

13

THE DORMOUSE'S TALE

After forty days and forty nights the rain—which God had sent to destroy the earth and all its wickedness—had stopped. The flood waters had gone down and the ark was grounded on the top of a mountain called Ararat.

The animals, insects and birds who had shared the ark with Mr Noah and his family for so long were all ready to leave. They crowded into the big hall, noisy and excited.

'Where's Mr Noah?' asked the goat irritably. 'Why doesn't he come and open the door?'

'Yes,' said the wolf licking his lips. 'I want to get out of here and go hunting again.'

The fox grinned and eyed the rabbits and the dormice thoughtfully.

'Mmm... tasty... very tasty... but which to eat first?'

'It's so hard to make decisions, isn't it?' said the panther softly as he paced up and down. The jackal laughed, showing sharp teeth.

The dormouse and his wife listened to this talk and shivered.

Mr Noah, in the meantime, was still in his cabin, slowly packing his things and talking to God.

'You know I didn't want to take the job on in the first place, God, and I must admit that at times I didn't think we'd make it, but now it's all over I feel quite sad.'

'It isn't all over yet, Noah,' God said.

'Isn't it?'

'Not quite.'

There was a knock and the lion entered. He had washed and brushed his mane and looked quite splendid..

'Ah, Mr Noah, forgive me for interrupting but everyone's waiting.'

'Waiting?'

'For you to open the door—unless of course God himself honours us with his presence.'

Mr Noah got to his feet.

'Of course,' he said. 'How stupid of me. I didn't think you'd all be quite so eager to go. I must come and say goodbye.'

The lion bowed himself out.

'I see what you mean, God, about it not being over,' Mr Noah said. 'I'm shirking my duties.'

God smiled, but said nothing.

Mr Noah left his cabin and closed the door behind

him. He was a short man with rounded shoulders bent with age. His beard had grown long during the voyage and his robe was shabby and much mended. He did not look at all important. He slowly made his way along the corridor and entered the big hall. When they saw him, all the animals and insects stood up and cheered. The birds flew down from the rafters and, at a signal from the blackbird, burst into song.

'Three cheers for Mr Noah!' quacked the duck, and the noise echoed through the ark. Mr Noah stopped still in

amazement. He looked round the hall and tears came to his eyes.

The cheers ended in a storm of clapping. Tails thumped on the floor, birds flapped their wings and the elephant did a short dance with the kangaroo. Mr Noah held up his hand for silence.

'My dear friends,' he began, but his voice was quite choked. He cleared his throat and started again. 'My *very* dear friends. This is altogether too kind of you. Much too kind. But you shouldn't cheer me, you know. I just did what God told me. He's the one who saved you from the flood.'

'But you made it possible,' said the lion. He stepped forwards in a dignified manner and coughed importantly. 'Hmph, her-umph... Mr Noah, on behalf of all the creatures of the world...'

'Cut the cackle and open the door,' called the fox rudely.

The lion ignored him. 'On this most important, indeed illustrious, occasion...'

'What's he talking about?' asked the giraffe.

'... I take it upon myself as your assistant and King of all the Animals...'

'Watch it,' said the tiger dangerously.

'... to offer our deepest thanks to Mr Noah, Mrs Noah, their sons Shem, Ham and Japheth and their sons' most charming wives...'

The crocodile yawned loudly.

'...for saving us from the flood. We animals...'

'He doesn't mean us, dear, we're not animals, I'm pleased to say,' said the cockroach to his wife.

'We animals...'

A chant began at the back of the hall.

'Open the door, *open the door*, OPEN THE DOOR...!'

It grew louder and the lion, looking rather put out, stopped speaking.

'Thank you, lion, for those kind thoughts,' said Mr Noah hurriedly. 'You and the tiger have both been very good and faithful assistants. Now,' he said in a louder voice. 'Before I open the door and we go our separate ways, I need to cross your names off my list.'

'Why do you need to do that?' asked the goose. 'We're all here, same as when we started, apart from the doves of course.'

'I like to keep things straight,' said Mr Noah.

So, with a certain amount of grumbling and pushing, the animals, insects and birds formed into a queue.

'All this red tape is very tiring,' grumbled the goose.

'Well, I think it's excellent,' said the magpie fussily. 'These things should be checked.'

'To make sure you haven't been stealing bits of the ark, I suppose,' the monkey said sourly.

'Well, really...!' The magpie bristled.

'Oh dear,' said the ostrich. 'I think I can feel one of my

headaches coming on.'

At last the checking was completed.

'Well,' said Mr Noah, putting a large cross beside a name. 'That seems to be that. I just want to say goodbye, good luck for the future and may God bless you all.' He made his way to the stout door. 'Now ...'

'Wait a minute, Father.' Japheth came hurrying up, waving his list in his hand. 'Wait a minute. There's two animals missing.'

'Missing?'

'Yes. The dormice aren't here.'

'They're not animals, they're rodents,' said the fox.

Mr Noah turned and called out loudly, 'Are the dormice anywhere in the hall?'

There was silence.

He tried again. 'Has anybody seen the dormice?'

'No, but I'd like to,' said the fox, grinning and licking his lips.

'We'd better search the ark.'

The search lasted for some time. The animals, insects and birds went everywhere, calling the dormice by name and peering into the smallest of holes, but it was Mr Noah who found them cowering inside a cupboard in his cabin.

Mr Noah stared down at them.

'Whatever are you doing here? Don't you know we've been searching for you?'

'W-w-well ...' stammered one of the dormice.

'It's like this ...' the other began.

Mr Noah sighed. 'You can't stay there in the cupboard. Come along to the big hall. All the animals are anxious to get away.'

'Yes,' said the first dormouse. 'That's just it. They want to get away so they can begin hunting again and the first thing they'll hunt is us.'

'That's nonsense,' said Mr Noah.

'No, it isn't. We heard them talking in the hall just now, about how nice it would be to go hunting again. That fox had his eye on us and so did some of the other animals. I don't think we'll last two minutes once we're off this ark.'

The dormice were shaking with fright.

'I see,' said Mr Noah slowly. He sat on the bed. 'But surely it won't be like that, not now you've all got to know each other? I can't believe the other animals would want to eat you.'

'Not only the animals,' said the first dormouse. 'That eagle had a very nasty glint in his eye.'

'We've been dreading this day,' confessed the second dormouse. 'It's kept us awake at night, worrying.'

'Well, I'm very sorry ...' began Mr Noah.

'You see, we've really enjoyed it here,' said the first dormouse. 'We've been cared for and looked after and you've no idea what a relief it's been not to have to worry

about finding food for ourselves...'

'... or being eaten by others,' chimed in the second dormouse.

'We've *mattered*. You've listened to us when we've talked and sometimes the bigger animals have listened too. It's been so safe here. Safe and friendly. We just don't want to go. Please, can't we stay?'

'Can't we?' added the second dormouse.

They looked up at him with pleading faces.

'I don't know what to say,' said Mr Noah. 'All I've thought about was keeping you safe during this trip. I never thought about the future.' He put his head in his hands. 'Perhaps that was what you meant, God, when you said it wasn't all over.' He looked at the dormice. 'Go back to the hall and wait for me there. I've got to think about this, and talk to God.'

The dormice looked at one another. 'I think we'd rather stay here in this cupboard, if you don't mind.'

'It's safer,' agreed the other dormouse.

'But none of the animals will harm you on the ark,' said Mr Noah.

'They'll be pretty angry with us for the delay,' the first dormouse said and shivered.

'All right,' said Mr Noah. 'But just be quiet a minute while I talk this over with God.'

'We'll be quiet as mice,' said the dormouse with an anxious smile.

'What shall I do, God?' Mr Noah asked. 'Have I kept the animals safe on the ark only for them to be eaten as soon as they go outside?'

'Your part is finished once they leave the ark, Noah,' God replied. 'I did not ask you to do anything else.'

'Yes, but I can't just let them go to their deaths,' argued Mr Noah. 'I mean, what would have been the point of keeping them safe all these weeks?'

'You are not responsible for them, Noah. I am. Can't you trust me?'

'I do, Lord,' said Mr Noah. He looked up. 'But I still feel responsible,' he added.

God smiled. 'You are a faithful servant, Noah, and I am very fond of you, but you cannot take the weight of the world and all its problems on your shoulders.'

'No, Lord. But surely I can do *something*.'

God considered for a moment. 'Very well. Go back to the hall and tell all the animals, insects and birds what has happened.'

Mr Noah stood up and went over to the cupboard.

'Come along,' he said. 'We're going to the big hall and I'm going to tell the animals, insects and birds what you told me.'

'Is that wise?' asked the dormouse.

'It's what God suggests,' said Mr Noah. He looked down at the two dormice who were still shivering with fright. 'And don't be frightened. We're all in God's hands and he will protect you.'

The dormice came out of the cupboard and went with Mr Noah to the big hall. And for the last time Mr Noah called together a meeting of all the creatures in the ark.

14

THE END OF THE VOYAGE

It was very quiet in the big hall as Mr Noah stepped forwards and told the animals, insects and birds that the two dormice were afraid to leave the ark for fear they would be eaten.

When he had finished speaking the fox said angrily, 'It's a load of rubbish!'

'No, it's not,' said the dormouse. 'We *are* frightened. Some of you would snap us up in an instant if it weren't for Mr Noah.'

'Hear, hear!' said the ant. 'You're not the only ones to be frightened about leaving. We're scared too.'

'So are we!' called the rabbits.

At this there was uproar in the hall. Some of the animals were shouting agreement and others were roaring them down.

'Quiet!' Mr Noah shouted.

The fox jumped on to a table. 'You don't want to be taken in, Mr Noah! Those dormice would tell you anything to get your sympathy!' He thumped his tail loudly. 'I tell you, they're not worth saving! Why, if they weren't kept down, they'd be over-running the world! Vermin, that's what they are!'

'There's no need to be rude!' squeaked the dormouse and the animals, insects and birds all began shouting once more.

'QUIET!' roared Mr Noah. 'QUIET!! Haven't you learned *anything* on this voyage? I had thought—I had *hoped*—that you would have learned to understand and respect each other a little during the time we've been together.'

'Very true,' said the donkey, nodding his head. 'I've learnt that there are an awful lot of animals in the world beside myself.'

'Shush, dear,' said his wife. 'I don't think Mr Noah meant that.'

'I think Mr Noah's got a point,' the beaver said slowly. 'While we've been on this ark we've all had to face the same danger. We've got on pretty well on the whole and it would be sad to think that everything we've learned would be lost when we go out into the world.'

'What do you suggest we do about it?' asked the camel.

'I don't know,' said the beaver.

'Well, I suggest we should stop all this chatter and get out of the ark,' said the jackal impatiently. 'Anyone would

think you *liked* being here.'

'That's just the point,' said the dormouse earnestly. 'Some of us *do* like it here. At least, I'm sure we'd all rather be in the fresh air again, but some of us like feeling safe, and we do feel safe on the ark.'

'Mr Noah, what do you think?' asked the hedgehog.

'I don't know,' said Mr Noah slowly. 'But if God found the world so wicked that he had to destroy it, then surely those of us he saved from the flood should try to make the new world a better place.'

'Impossible,' said the monkey sarcastically.

'Perhaps I should remind you that it wasn't *our* wickedness that caused God to flood the world,' said the eagle. 'You humans are to blame, not us.'

'I don't know,' said the dormouse. 'It's very easy to blame others, but nobody's perfect, whatever you say.'

The eagle glared at him. 'Just you wait,' he hissed.

'But what can we *do*?' asked the jackal impatiently.

There was silence in the hall. Then the donkey spoke. 'I've got an idea,' he said slowly. 'I know I'm a bit stupid, but I *have* got an idea. Please listen to it.'

'Do you think you should, dear?' asked his wife.

The donkey took a deep breath and began. 'It is right, isn't it, Mr Noah, that we are the only creatures left in the world?' he asked.

'Quite right.'

'So my wife and I are the only two donkeys left?'

'Yes.'

'And God saved us so that there will always be donkeys in the world?'

The jackal yawned loudly.

'That's true.'

'So it must be important to God that we survive, not just on the ark but when we're off it as well?'

'Well, yes,' said Mr Noah.

'In that case, why don't we all agree that none of us who have been on the ark will hunt or eat each other?'

The monkey scratched himself noisily. 'Now I've heard it all!' he said in a sarcastic voice.

The donkey looked round the big hall. 'We could form ourselves into a sort of league and agree that, as long as we are alive, we will not harm one another.'

There was silence. The animals, insects and birds looked at one another, suspiciously, doubtingly, warily... hopefully.

'Do you think it would work?' asked the hedgehog.

'I don't know,' said the donkey. He shrugged, rather embarrassed at the attention he was getting. 'It's only an idea and I know I'm not very good at ideas...'

'I think it's a very good idea,' said Mr Noah.

'So do I,' said the dormouse.

'And I'll vote for it,' said the tiger loudly. 'All those in favour?'

There was a roar of agreement.

'Now,' said the tiger briskly, 'we need someone to be the first Head of our new United League of Animals, Insects and Birds...'

'Do we?' asked the goose.

'Of course we do,' said the tiger. 'Every organization has to have someone in charge. Are there any suggestions?'

'Well,' said the lion. 'Ah, hmm... well...'

'The lion?' suggested the goose. 'After all, he is King of the Jungle.'

The lion smiled graciously at the goose.

'Personally I always thought the lion dreamed up that title for himself,' said the tiger huffily.

'Well, what about you?' suggested the panther.

'I don't mind,' said the tiger modestly.

'I suggest the bear,' snapped the lion. 'Brawn before brains and he's the strongest animal among us.'

'Why do we need a *Head* anyway?' murmured the

squirrel.' *Tails* are far more important.' He waved his fine one in the air.

'I think it should be the donkey,' said the dormouse. 'After all, he came up with the idea in the first place.'

'Oh no,' said the donkey, shaking his head. 'I couldn't do it. I'm much too stupid.'

'Why should it be an animal, anyway?' asked the cockroach. 'Why not an insect? Animals always like to push themselves forwards.'

'Why not a bird?' asked the seagull. 'The eagle would have my vote.'

'The owl is the wisest,' said the falcon.

The animals, insects and birds all began speaking at once.

'If we can't even agree on someone to be the Head of our new league, what *can* we agree on?' asked the donkey sadly.

The monkey smiled in a superior way. 'These things never work,' he said to no one in particular.

'Can I suggest Mr Noah?' said the dormouse. 'He is neither an animal, an insect or a bird and he's kept us safe during this voyage. I would rather have him than one of us.'

'But what do I have to do?' asked Mr Noah.

'Look after us in the world,' said the dormouse.

The animals, insects and birds quietened down and looked at Mr Noah expectantly.

'What shall I do, God?' Mr Noah asked. 'It's a big

responsibility.'

'It is indeed,' said God. 'But one that is right. I give all the creatures of the world into your hands. Look after them well.'

Mr Noah was silent for a moment.

'Very well,' he said at last. 'If that is what you want me to do, God.' He raised his voice. 'If that is what you all want, then I accept the charge and I and my sons will try to look after you and keep you from harm.'

'Well then,' said the fox brightly. 'Now we're all friends together I think Mr Noah should open the door and let us out.'

Mr Noah turned to the dormouse. 'Are you any happier?' he asked.

'Yes,' said the dormouse after a moment's thought.

'I think so.'

'Very well then.'

Mr Noah went to the big door that God himself had closed at the start of the journey. It opened at his touch and sunlight streamed into the hall.

And Mr Noah led the animals, insects and birds out of the ark. There were wild animals, tame animals, reptiles and insects, birds and beasts. There were large animals and small animals, ugly and good-looking ones. There were animals with nice natures and animals with nasty natures. Two of every kind had gone into the ark and two of every kind—apart from the doves—came out of the ark to stand with Mr Noah on the green grass and look with wonder at the fresh new world around them.

Then the birds rose into the air like a cloud, circling

Mr Noah and his family as they called their goodbyes. Mr Noah lifted his hands and blessed them and they flew away.

'Goodbye,' said the skunks and slunk off among the trees.

'Goodbye,' said the termites as they abandoned their home on the ark and wriggled away.

'Goodbye,' grunted the pigs as they set off in search of food.

'Goodbye, goodbye,' called all the animals and insects as they went their own ways out of the clearing and into the wood.

'It's been an experience,' said the lion grandly as he offered his paw for Mr Noah to shake.

'Thank you and goodbye,' said the spiders shyly and waved their long legs.

Mr Noah stood and watched them all go.

'Goodbye and God bless you,' he called.

'Well,' said the fox. 'Good hunting.' He winked and made a playful grab at the dormouse, laughing out loud as the dormouse squeaked in fright.

'Only teasing,' he said and swaggered off.

Mr Noah watched until the last of the animals had gone, then he and his family thanked God for having brought them all safely through the flood.

'Will they keep their promise to each other, God?' he asked.

'For a while,' God said.

'And will we keep our promise to care for them?'

'*You* will, Noah,' God replied.

The sunlit day grew overcast and a few drops of rain began to fall.

'Are you starting the flood again, Lord?' Mr Noah asked humbly.

'No,' said God. 'For whatever promises are made and broken, this *I* promise. I will never again destroy all living things by water and never again shall there be a flood to destroy the earth.'

The rain fell harder and Mr Noah stared miserably at the wet ground.

'Cheer up, Noah,' said God. 'Look up at the sky.'

Mr Noah looked up and there, high above him, he saw the perfect arc of a rainbow, its colours glowing as the sun burst through the clouds—red, orange, yellow, green, blue, indigo and violet.

'This rainbow is my promise to you and to all who live after you,' said God. 'Whenever you see a rainbow in the sky you will think of my promise and know that I will never again send a flood to destroy the earth. And, Noah...'

'Yes, Lord?'

'Remember that *I* do not break my promises.'

'No, Lord,' said Mr Noah.

Then, as the rain stopped and the sun shone warm on

his face, Mr Noah looked around at his wife, his three sons, Shem, Ham and Japheth and their wives.

'Funny,' he said, 'but it seems lonely without the animals. I shall miss them.' He sighed. 'I must admit I've grown rather fond of them.'

'Even the spiders?' asked God.

Mr Noah smiled. 'Especially the spiders,' he said.

RIVERBANK STORIES

Stephen Lawhead

Two delightful and amusing tales set in the watery world of Oxford's rivers. Happy with their peaceful riverbank life, Jeremy Vole and Anabelle Hedgehog don't go looking for excitement, but each one is drawn into an unexpected and sometimes surprising adventure.

'Compelling reading for younger readers.'
The School Librarian

THE TALE OF JEREMY VOLE
ISBN 0-7459-1653-8

THE TALE OF ANABELLE HEDGEHOG
ISBN-0-7459-1924-3

Mrs. Noah's Rainy Day Book

Sue Atkinson

- What is the world's smallest mammal?
- How can you make rain in your kitchen?
- Which animal can run the farthest?
- What are the colors of the rainbow?

You can find the answers and much, much more in *Mrs. Noah's Rainy Day Book*.

Former teacher and writer Sue Atkinson has used all her experience and creativity to bring the familiar Bible story of Noah and his ark to life for children today. Her imaginative retelling of this story is only the beginning.

There are puzzles and quizzes about he animal world and conservation, simple science projects and fun facts about the weather, the 'Rainbow' board game, and much more.

This fun-packed activity book will entertain 7-11 year olds come rain or shine.

ISBN 0-7459-2375-5